His hand cupped hers, which was still resting on his arm.

"I hear you're a great cook. Anytime you want to cook for us will be appreciated."

She hadn't realized she was still touching him. Her pulse pounding through her body, she stepped back. "I'll take that under consideration." Cody rattled her.

Maggie watched him a moment as he made his way outside to help with docking the boat, then realized she was staring. She averted her gaze but discovered that Kim was studying her from across the cabin. Her cousin raised her eyebrows, a smirk on her face. Oh, great. She'd never hear the end of it now.

Kim was out to fix up all single people in Hope, just like Maggie's boss. Matchmaking was contagious obviously. Maggie turned to Ruth and caught her looking at her, too. Double whammy. She could see the wheels turning in both women's minds.

It might be a long afternoon.

Books by Margaret Daley

MARGARET DALEY

feels she has been blessed. She has been married more than thirty years to her husband, Mike, whom she met in college. He is a terrific support and her best friend. They have one son, Shaun. Margaret has been writing for many years and loves to tell a story. When she was a little girl, she would play with her dolls and make up stories about their lives. Now she writes these stories down. She especially enjoys weaving stories about families and how faith in God can sustain a person when things get tough. When she isn't writing, she is fortunate to be a teacher for students with special needs. Margaret has taught for more than twenty years and loves working with her students. She has also been a Special Olympics coach and has participated in many sports with her students.

A Mom's New Start

Margaret Daley

Love Inspired

 ™ LOVE INSPIRED BOOKS

Recycling programs
for this product may
not exist in your area.

ISBN-13: 978-0-373-81645-3

A MOM'S NEW START

Copyright © 2012 by Margaret Daley

www.LoveInspiredBooks.com

Printed in U.S.A.

For thou art my hope, O Lord God;
thou art my trust from my youth.
—*Psalms* 71:5

For Catherine and Tony David, who lived through several hurricanes and helped others rebuild.

Chapter One

"Hold the elevator," Maggie Sommerfield called out, rushing toward it while juggling three sacks full of heavy books.

With a glance at the wall clock near the stairs she usually took to City Hall's third floor, she noted her timing was worse than she thought. Now she was going to be late to Bienville to help set up the belated wedding reception for her boss and mayor, Ruth Sommerfield, and her uncle Keith. Her cousin, Kim, who was hosting the party with her, wasn't going to be happy. She should have waited until later to bring the books to City Hall.

Committed now, Maggie stepped onto the elevator and immediately set her sacks on the tiled floor, her arms beginning to ache from holding them so long. When she looked up into the face of the only other occupant, her gaze met Cody Weston's amused smile.

Seeing him surprised Maggie because it was Saturday evening. She guessed, though, being a psychologist and counselor with the Christian Assistance Coalition here in Hope, Mississippi, helping the victims of Hurricane Naomi meant he worked whatever hours his clients needed him. It certainly had been the case when he had worked with her uncle Keith with his post-traumatic stress disorder after the disastrous storm. Her uncle had spent most of his time in his bedroom, retreating from others, but now he was happy and in love with Ruth. Thanks to Cody.

"I've never seen a woman with so many books. Are those for the Ultimate Garage Sale in two weeks?" Cody asked, lounging back against the wall.

"Yes, my last load. I think I could have re-stocked the local library with the books I had, but they prefer hardbacks and so many of mine are paperbacks. But Mrs. Abare had tons of hard-backs and I mean tons." She rubbed her arms, suddenly conscious of being alone with a man she had admired from a distance.

"I'm assuming you're going to the third floor?"

"Yes." They both worked on the top floor of City Hall, one of the historical buildings that survived the category-four hurricane eight months ago—a storm that still left over a third of the town recovering from the destruction.

The elevator, which Maggie was sure was an antique, slowly began the ascent to the top floor where she worked as the secretary to the mayor and town council. A grinding sound echoed through the cab right before the elevator came to a stop.

Between the second and third floor.

Maggie froze, waiting a few heartbeats for the elevator to continue its journey.

It didn't.

She hit every button on the console, jabbing them with urgency. Nothing.

"It's stuck." Cody paused then added, "Again."

"What do you mean *again?* Have there been problems?"

"It usually gets stuck at least once a day lately."

"Why didn't someone tell me? I knew I should have used the stairs. The one time I don't…" Her words rushed to a halt, and she swallowed several times to coat her suddenly dry throat. On top of that, sweat popped out on her forehead, a rivulet running down into her eye, and her heart raced. Before long the walls would begin to press in on her, and she would hyperventilate.

"Let me guess. You're afraid of confined spaces."

"Yes," she bit out, trying frantically to control her body's reaction to a fear she'd had all her life. She didn't want to fall apart in front of Cody, a man who seemed so together. "I believe, Dr. Weston, the term is claustrophobia."

"Yes, you're right."

"And it isn't so much confined spaces as a feeling of being trapped." The second she said the word "trapped" her thoughts zoomed back to when she had been eight and locked in an old root cellar for hours. Dark. Damp. Musky. All because a neighbor kid thought it was funny.

"They should have us out of here in no time."

Her gaze fastened on to the red button at the bottom of the console. *In case of an emergency.* She slammed her palm against it—a little too hard. Bells went off while her hand throbbed. "I should only work in one-story buildings." That realization didn't help her now. "Why did I have to clear out my car this evening? This could have waited until I had time to make more than one trip," she mumbled more to herself as she tried to focus on something other than being trapped. "Oh, no. It's Saturday. After six. Most people are gone by now. What if no one is in the building to hear the elevator alarm?"

She swept her attention to Cody, and immediately his calm seized her as if to assure her that she was safe. He was here to help her. In the midst of the loud ringing filling the cab, Maggie felt drawn to him as she had been when she'd seen him working with Uncle Keith, that same calm and patience evident time after time. For an instant she forgot where she was as she continued to stare at Cody. Too bad he was only in town for a short time.

The alarm ceased.

She pushed away her attraction to a man who only had, at the most, a couple months left in town and latched on to the hope that flared in her. "Good. Someone has turned it off." When Cody averted his gaze, her hope plummeted. "What's wrong?" He was avoiding eye contact. Never a good thing in an emergency.

"It automatically goes off after a certain time."

"How do you know that?"

"I was stuck in this elevator earlier in the week."

"And you got back on it? What are you, crazy?"

He shrugged. "I like to live dangerously."

She didn't want to hear that. "Okay. Do you have a cell phone? I left mine in my purse in my car. I was only gonna be in here a few minutes."

He cocked a grin. "Sorry. That's why I was going back upstairs. Forgot it on my desk."

The urge to pound on the doors and yell for

help inundated Maggie. She didn't think her heart rate could go any faster, but it did. Its sound thundered against her skull. Surely he could hear it, too. She looked at the top of the elevator at the escape hatch. Maybe if she got on his shoulders, he could hoist her through....

"Aren't you hosting the party tonight at Bienville?"

His question came to her through a fog of desperation. "Huh?"

"The belated wedding reception tonight for your uncle and the mayor?"

His question refocused her attention on him. Cody went from one disaster to another. That was his job. His expression even, not an ounce of fear in it, he looked back at her. He exuded calm, control this whole time. Two things she didn't.

"Maggie?"

The unflappable way he spoke her name centered her on him a few feet away from her. "Yes, I'm hosting it with Kim and her husband."

He moved closer, cutting the meager distance between them in half. "Why were you bringing books to your office then?"

It was his nearness this time that caused her heart to beat even faster. "For Ellie, the DA. She's the organizer for the town garage sale for the library," she replied when she realized all she was doing was staring at him.

"Well, then she's in the building and heard the alarm."

"Not exactly. I needed my trunk space so I thought I would drop them off here. She has a vacant room on the third floor down the hall from my office. That's where she's storing the books until the garage sale. I have a key to it." Maggie checked her watch. "She's probably getting ready for the party right now." Panic began to swirl around in her stomach. Words that flooded her mind a few seconds ago vanished.

She spied the emergency button and punched it again. The alarm blasted the air. She glanced around, and it seemed the elevator had shrunk. Was it this small a minute ago? She gulped in air, but nothing she did filled her lungs.

Her gaze latching on to the escape door in the ceiling, she waved her hand. "You can hoist me up there. I'll see if I can reach the third floor door and pry it open. I've seen it done in movies."

"Maggie."

She peered at him, now only a foot away from her. His handsome features set in a composed countenance, he took her hand still wildly gesturing at the ceiling. The blue in his eyes, like the Gulf not far from Bienville, drew her toward him. The gleam in them reminded her of sunlight glittering off the surface of the water.

"Tell me about the books you have in those sacks."

"Books?"

"The ones for the garage sale."

"Oh," she muttered, transfixed by the smile on his face creating two dimples in his cheeks. She'd never noticed that before. No, that wasn't right. She had but she'd refused to dwell on how much they appealed to her. "I collected these from Mrs. Abare today. I've already given Ellie mine."

"What do you like to read?"

Heat flushed her face. "Romance."

One eyebrow arched. "You do? I like a good mystery myself."

"You're kidding."

"Nope." He still held her hand between them, his warmth against her cold fingers soothing.

For five whole seconds she didn't even think about where she was. "I haven't really read many mysteries." Then she slid her gaze toward the control panel.

"Maggie." He said her name in a husky voice. It lured her back to him. "I'll loan you one of my books."

She inhaled a composing breath that seemed

to be working. "In that case, I'll loan you one of my books and we can compare."

He chuckled. "A romance?"

"Why not? I've always said men should read them to learn how women think about what love is."

"Okay. I'm game."

"You are?"

Those two dimples deepened as his smile grew. "I'm willing to try and figure out what women want. It might help me in my work."

"Yes, it could. Think of it as research."

"Yeah, research." He laughed again and pressed on. "How's your son doing now that it's summer?"

"According to Brady, it's gonna be a long, boring summer. He is usually so busy with his friends I don't hear that until a few days before school starts at the end of August. Not this year, but then he's gonna be thirteen soon."

"Aah, such a fun time. It wasn't that long ago for me."

The subject of her son reminded her of the stress she'd endured for the past month, concerning Brady. That stress reinforced the situation she was in at the moment. She peered at the emergency button again, trying to decide if hitting it a third time would make it work any better.

"How are Keith and Ruth?"

Suddenly the elevator began moving upward. The unexpected jolt sent her flying against him. He clasped her upper arms and steadied her. The whisper of his breath caressed her cheek before he pulled back, giving her some room. But it wasn't enough. Not even clear across town would be enough. Her mouth went ever drier as her pulse sped through her body.

"See. We're being rescued," he said as the elevator stopped and the doors swished open.

A blush still scorched her face. The scent of peppermint on his breath lingered, teasing her senses. Touching a part of her that she'd closed off when her fiancé died thirteen and a half years ago. When he was killed, she'd thought part of herself had died, too. No man was going to change that feeling. And certainly not a man who was only here a short time. She needed to remember that and keep her distance from Cody.

For a few seconds she didn't move until he nudged her forward, saying, "I'll get your books for you."

Finally she scurried off, looking around for the person responsible for rescuing them. No one was in the corridor. "Hello," she called.

Nothing.

Cody stepped off the elevator with all three

bags of books. "Maybe it fixed itself. It's a contrary elevator."

"One I will never ride again. I don't care what I have to carry up the stairs."

"Where can I put these?"

"Here let me take one." She approached him, again vividly aware of his nearness.

"Naw. I've got this. Just show me where to take them."

"This way." She walked toward a door at the far end, the click of her heels echoing through the hallway.

"If you know you have trouble with confined spaces, why did you get on the elevator?"

She could now get back to normal, put the incident on the elevator behind her. "A spur of the moment decision which I regret. That should teach me to stop doing things suddenly and without thought. But I'm wearing heels, and I don't usually. I saw the staircase and wasn't sure I could make it all the way up with the sacks. It's been a long day getting everything ready for my uncle's wedding reception. The whirlwind romance between Uncle Keith and Ruth is the one thing good that came from the hurricane. I don't know if they would have gotten together otherwise." She was chattering, which had to be a result of her nervous state due to the elevator incident—certainly not the man nearby. Okay, maybe it was because of the man beside her.

Cody nodded. "Ruth was what Keith needed. She gave him something to focus on other than the damage caused by the hurricane. The whole town is excited about the marriage."

"Yeah, everyone has contributed to the reception. Ellie did the flower arrangements. Mrs. Abare the cake. If it hadn't been for Mrs. Abare giving me the books this afternoon when I went to pick up the cake—" She clapped her hand over her mouth.

"What's wrong?"

"The cake is out in the car. The icing could have melted while we were trapped in the elevator." She hurried her pace, pulling the key to the storage room out of her pocket.

"We were only in the elevator ten minutes."

Only ten minutes? It had seemed much longer, until she'd centered on Cody, then time just seemed to melt away. "Good. Then there's hope the cake is fine," she finally said as she opened the door and he set the sacks on the table in the room.

"In a town called Hope, there should be." The six-foot-tall counselor closed the door and locked it.

"True, but since Hurricane Naomi, it has been

scarce." She headed for the stairs in the center of the corridor. "I can't thank you enough for help-ing my uncle. He's a new man since you started counseling him."

At the top of the staircase he stopped, a smile sparkling in his blue eyes. Again a vision of the water on a clear day pushed into her thoughts. She could get used to looking into those eyes everyday, but she didn't have any time to get involved in anyone else's life. Brady had to be paramount in her life; in fact, he would always come first.

"I have to give Ruth a lot of the credit. She gives Keith a reason to get up in the morning," Cody said, as though his part was nothing.

So many men she knew would be taking full credit for her uncle's recovery but not Cody, which only gave her another reason to like him. "How much longer are you going to stay in Hope?" she asked, as if to reinforce why she needed to keep her distance.

"A few more months. My caseload is still heavy. A lot of people have had trouble dealing with the hurricane."

"It was a category-four storm, but I think part of the reason it's hit us hard was the way it kept toying with the town. It was heading for us, then it wasn't, then it was. People's emotions took a ride that week."

He tilted his head to the side, his hand on the ornate railing. "But from what I've seen, you've weathered it well."

She hadn't thought he had noticed her much. Other than casual conversations occasionally, she'd kept herself in the background. "I didn't have a home to lose."

"What about Bienville?"

"It belongs to my uncle and his family. Although he and Kim have been wonderful to me and my son, it's not mine." Yet Bienville was her home, especially when her mother turned her back on her right after her fiancé had died and she had discovered she was pregnant with Brady. Uncle Keith had given her a place to live and had helped her rebuild her life. She owed him a lot.

"And that bothers you?"

She took a step back and nearly went down the stairs. Clutching the railing near his hand, she glanced over her shoulder. "What do you mean by that?" she asked in a breathless voice, not feeling bothered but obliged to her uncle and his family.

"I hear regret in your voice."

"You're mistaken." She had no regrets about Bienville but she did regret the mistakes she'd made in her life that had alienated her from her immediate family, especially her father who had supported her mother's decision. She and her mother had never been very close, but she'd had a good relationship with her dad until she'd become pregnant with Brady. Now her mother was dead, and any chance to reconcile with her was gone. Eighteen months ago her mother had passed away from a heart attack. Her dad had called her from Sedona to tell her after the funeral.

"If you say so."

"I do." Yes, in the past Bienville had been important to her—a tie to her family, a place where she and Brady could put down roots. She shifted away from Cody before he read something in her expression she didn't want him to see. He was perceptive, which was probably why he was so good at his job. But she didn't need to be psycho-analyzed. She'd gotten over being abandoned by her mother a long time ago. "I'd better get moving or Kim will wonder where I went. My quick errand to get the cake has turned into a marathon trip." She chuckled. "But that shouldn't surprise my cousin."

"See you later."

At the bottom of the third-floor steps she looked up at him. "Don't tell anyone about the elevator incident. My family thinks I've overcome my fear."

"If they find out, it has to come from you."

She continued her trip down to the first floor, resisting the urge to look at him again. She felt his gaze on her until she disappeared from his view. Goose bumps prickled her skin from head to toe.

When Maggie arrived at her car, she sighed. The cake icing had not melted. Maybe the reception would be a success, after all. She wanted it to be. Uncle Keith, Kim and Kim's ten-year-old daughter, Anna, were more family than her father and younger brother were. She hadn't seen either one in years.

Ten minutes later, she pulled into the drive that led to Bienville. The renovations due to the hurricane were almost complete. The outside looked good—better than it had before the hurricane. The only remnants of the storm's damage were evident in parts of the downstairs, still being remodeled. Soon Uncle Keith and Ruth would move into the master bedroom on the first floor, leaving the upstairs for Maggie and Brady. Almost like it had been before the hurricane, except that Kim and Anna had lived upstairs with them then. But now that her cousin had married Zane Davidson, Kim and her daughter lived at his place outside of town. She missed having Kim, who was like a younger sister to her, living at Bienville, but they did see each other a lot. That was one of the reasons she loved living in Hope. She didn't have to go far to run into a friend or a member of her extended family.

Carefully grasping the tray the three-tiered cake sat on, Maggie started up the rear steps. When she was nearly at the top that led to the gallery of the antebellum house, the door to the game room slammed open then closed. She peered around the cake a few seconds before her son, his head down, nearly collided into her. Swinging the cake out over the railing, she avoided a catastrophe as he breezed by her on the steps.

"Hey, Brady. Stop. Where are you going?" Maggie brought the cake back toward her chest, steadying the plate. She'd had visions of the three tiers tumbling to the ground below.

He halted at the bottom and rotated toward her. "Out."

"The party is in an hour."

"Kinda hard not to know that when everyone is running around."

The exasperation in her son's voice needled her. Nothing pleased him of late. "Have you helped?"

"Sure. What's the big deal anyway? It's just a party."

"It's a time for us to celebrate your uncle getting married."

Brady frowned, his mouth pinched together.

"C'mon. I'm sure we can use your help with last-minute preparations."

"I *am* helping. Kim asked me to go get Anna at her friend's house next door." He turned on his heel and hurried away.

Even from several yards away, Maggie felt the frost of her son's words. He was nearly thirteen, and although he loved Uncle Keith, she doubted he was thrilled with coming to a party with mostly adults. This was just a phase he was going through. In a few years he would grow out of it and—

Who was she kidding? He wasn't even a full-fledged teenager, and he was already moody and difficult to be around.

Maggie opened the back door. Inside, the blast of air-conditioning cooled off her hot cheeks and sweat-coated forehead.

Entering the game room, she spied Kim and Zane finishing up last-minute preparations to the buffet table. "I've got the cake," Maggie announced when her cousin looked up.

"I was beginning to worry about you." Kim

patted the white tablecloth where she wanted Maggie to set the cake.

"I told her you didn't skip town and leave her to finish up all by herself." Zane started for the door out to the upstairs landing.

"I'd never do that." Maggie put down the tray on the table. "Where are you going?"

"I'm leaving the rest to you two. I was just filling in for you until you showed up. I'm all thumbs when it comes to decorating."

"That's no excuse to leave us shorthanded." Kim balled her hand and settled it on her hip.

As Zane left the room, Uncle Keith came into it. "I can help if you need a hand."

Kim waved him off. "Shoo. This is supposed to be a surprise. I thought you and Ruth were resting. You are not to come in here until seven-thirty. Not one minute before. We went to a lot of trouble to keep this a secret."

"Not too much. Half the town has mentioned this 'surprise reception.'"

Maggie watched the loving exchange between Kim and her father, and Maggie's heart cracked a little bit. Brady would never have that. His father died before he was born, and no matter how many stories she told her son about Robbie, it wasn't the same thing. Being estranged from her own father made that clear to her. And now more than ever, her son could use a father to help him through the minefield of the teen years.

Later that evening at Bienville, the sun hid behind the tall pines and live oaks, cooling off June's muggy heat. Cody stood on the second-floor gallery staring at Keith's beautiful back-yard, such a change from five months ago when he was introduced to the Sommerfield family. At that time this place had looked like a war zone, and he supposed having a hurricane plow through the area was like being in the middle of a war.

Behind him he could hear the sounds of laughter and talking. The reception for Keith and Ruth was going full swing. The house was crammed with people celebrating their union. But as usual, he found he needed to escape for a while. He didn't often have to go to parties and that was fine by him. As a counselor he felt as though he had to be an extrovert, but deep inside he was the opposite. He cherished his alone time.

A vision of a very rattled Maggie Sommerfield caged in the elevator with him popped into his mind. A smile curved his mouth. For a moment he thought he smelled her scent of lavender—not a strong aroma but teasingly subtle. He'd kept smelling it long after she had left City Hall earlier this evening.

He'd actually grabbed his cell and rushed home to change and had shown up at Bienville precisely at seven-thirty. He never was one of the first to arrive at a party, but often he was one of the first to leave. The whole time he'd been here he couldn't get Maggie's look of vulnerability out of his mind. Being on the stalled elevator had really scared her. What if he hadn't been there? Who would have talked to her and calmed her?

The setting sun cast a rosy-orange color through the blue sky. The tranquility of the back-yard in contrast to the noise coming from the party beckoned him. After descending the steps, he walked toward the garden behind the antebel-lum house, pulling out his cell to reread Hannah's text. *Aaron left me. Call.*

He'd tried earlier before he'd arrived at the re-ception. Although behind the text he'd heard his younger sister's urgency, he wasn't surprised she wasn't home. Most likely her boyfriend got angry and went off to cool down. Everything was a cri-sis in Hannah's life. He'd learned to tone down her responses by half. It was never as bad as she thought.

One thing was for sure. She'd text back—even-tually.

Releasing a long sigh, he finally saw the array of flowers and foliage before him. Jasmine, hon-eysuckle, red, yellow, orange hibiscus bushes, a section of roses of various colors and big pink azaleas stretched before him. Their scents vied with the salty tang of the sea not far from Bienville. Seeing the beauty immediately eased his anxiety over Hannah and her latest "problem."

For this evening he would put Hannah's latest crisis on hold and enjoy one of his successes. Keith Sommerfield was a new man, full of hope and life after going through post-traumatic stress disorder following Hurricane Naomi. After the hours spent today counseling a suicidal client, he needed to see the good his work brought to others. This was what the Lord had called him to do. He would stay here a while longer, then move on to another disaster area.

He spied Maggie sitting on a wooden bench among the flowers. Her long brown hair caught the sunlight slanting through the leaves of a century-old live oak with Spanish moss draped on its branches. The rays tinted her hair a fiery hue, catching the red in it. She lifted her dark eyes and connected with his across the expanse of the garden. A smile slowly erased her troubled expression.

From what he had seen and heard when he'd arrived an hour ago, the reception was a success and the cake was intact on the center table. So why the frown? He moved toward her. He was used to helping others with their problems.

"It's nice to see you again," he said, pausing by a gardenia bush. Their aroma, a little too sweet for him, drove him farther into the garden. A birdbath invited several cardinals to drink, and they did even though Maggie sat on a bench only yards away.

"They're used to me. I usually come out here at this time of day. Right before the sun goes down. Old habits die hard."

"I doubt anyone will miss us. The place is packed. Ruth and Keith have a lot of friends."

"They've lived here all their lives."

"I wouldn't know what that means." Long ago he'd reconciled himself to the fact he wouldn't put down roots anywhere. He rarely stayed more than a year, usually only six or eight months. And as usual, his time would soon come to an end in Hope, too.

"I know your job takes you from one crisis to another, but did you also move a lot as a child?" Maggie scooted over to allow him to sit next to her.

"Yes. But Hope feels as close to a home-town as I've had. My father was assigned to the Keesler Air Force Base in Biloxi for two years when I was a kid. That was one of our longer stays in a town."

"So you're used to traveling and living in temporary places?"

"I don't know much else. How about you?"

"I've been here all my life. This is all I know. I can't imagine not being here."

There had been parts of always moving that he'd had to adjust to—like never really feeling a part of a place—but the rewards he received when he helped someone made up for that. He looked around at the colorful blossoms. "The hurricane had to affect this garden."

"It destroyed it."

"Who did this garden then?"

"Me, with some help from Kim's daughter, and Zane donated the plants."

Kim's new husband was as close to a friend as Cody allowed himself when he came to a new town to work. But always temporarily. He kept that in the back of his mind, especially after his failed attempt to keep a long-distance relationship going with Beth. He'd yearned for something more. He'd thought he could finally persuade Beth to change her life and follow him. He'd just started his mission when he'd met her and couldn't turn his back on it, but she didn't understand that. In the end they had parted. It had hurt deeply, only reinforcing his need to keep himself emotionally at a distance from others.

Shaking the past from his thoughts, Cody scanned the beauty around him. "That would have been about all I could do. Donate the plants." He held up his thumb. "Definitely not green."

"That's what I love about Bienville. It gives me a place to experiment and try different things. And Zane has been generous in letting me do that with these." Maggie spread her arm wide to indicate the plants. "I love seeing the beauty created by my efforts, especially from year to year."

He looked at the garden and had to agree at how rewarding something like this could be. But it wasn't for him. "Now that Kim and Zane are back from their honeymoon, he'll be starting the plans for the housing program he proposed to the Christian Assistance Coalition. I've been asked to work with him so it can be ready by late summer when hurricane season is in full swing."

"That's great. I'm sure y'all will do a wonderful job."

"Mostly Zane. I know nothing about building a house. I'm only the liaison between him and the organization for the time being. I think this will be a great benefit we can give financially strapped people who have lost their homes—a chance to rebuild with little or no cost to them."

"Like Zane has done in Hope."

"Yes, I know many of my clients have benefited from his generosity."

"Mom," Brady called from the second-floor gallery. "Uncle Keith and Aunt Ruth are getting ready to cut the cake."

"That's my cue to play hostess." Maggie rose. "If you've never had a piece of Mrs. Abare's cake, you're in for a treat."

"So I've heard." Cody pushed to his feet, hating to leave the tranquility of the garden, but loving celebrating his moment of triumph—Keith Sommerfield marrying and moving on with his life.

As they strolled toward the back steps, he slanted a look at Maggie. The last golden rays of the sun bathed her face in radiance. Her warm brown eyes captured his and for a few seconds he paused, enthralled by the woman he'd known casually for the past few months. She seemed so open, but he suspected there were many layers beneath the surface she didn't reveal to others. He did know one thing: she was grounded in her life in Hope while he'd purposefully stayed back as much as he could, preferring to be an observer rather than a participant.

At the steps he said, "After you," then followed her up to the back door that led into the game room. "When will Zane and his crew be finished with this house?"

"By the end of July. We may be family now, but there are so many people in worse need in Hope. He's hiring another crew so he can meet the demands. He seems to be doing that every few months."

"And I thought I worked long hours."

At the door she turned toward him. "You do. What were you doing at your office at six o'clock on Saturday?"

He laughed. "Catching up on work."

"See, what did I tell you? My job is just that. Work. I have too many other things I want to do with my life." She opened the door and entered the crowded room.

"Like what?"

"Being the best mom I can to Brady. That garden out there doesn't just happen, and I love to knit and read."

As Keith Sommerfield welcomed everyone to his home, Cody leaned close to Maggie and whispered, "I've heard about your prayer shawls."

"It's a great way to knit and help someone at the same time. When I get through with the needs in this town, I'll move on to the surrounding ones. I want everyone to be wrapped in God's love when they put on one of my shawls. They are given to people who need comfort and prayer." She weaved her way through the throng of people to get her camera for the cake cutting.

He liked how she thought. Why hadn't he noticed before? Because this assignment was temporary like all his others. It was better not to get emotional or notice someone he could be attracted to. That only made it harder to leave in the end, and he was afraid if he got too involved in Maggie's life, she would make him want to stay. Not good in the long run. Not after what he'd gone through with Beth.

As guests surged forward for a taste of the cake, Zane approached him. "What are you doing back here in the corner? Don't tell me you're going to escape before the party really gets going."

With an attempted suicide of one of his patients, it had been a long week. Cody was looking forward to doing nothing tomorrow except go to church then crash afterward. "Parties aren't my thing."

Zane's eyes widened. "I'm surprised you say that. You're always so at ease with people."

At a cost to himself. "I have to be or no one would tell me their worries."

"Personally I'm glad they do. What you did

for Keith was great. We actually have a relationship. Something I never thought would happen."

"The way you feel about Kim, I'm sure you would have found a way."

"Before you skip out, let's set up a meeting early next week to discuss the housing project."

"How about Wednesday?"

"The Fourth of July? You aren't working, are you?"

"I forgot that's next week. I don't have my calendar with me, but I'm sure I didn't plan anything for the Fourth."

A slow grin spread across Zane's face. "I've found someone who works as much as I do. Tell you what, we'll talk on the Fourth while we're on my boat. I'm taking the family out to Eagle Island. We'll be back in time to see the fireworks off the Point."

"I don't want to intrude." He particularly kept his distance with families. Sometimes he wished…

"Nonsense. You've been around enough to know we don't stand on ceremony. We'll be leaving bright and early. I'm not taking no for an answer. On the boat you'll actually be able to relax, and you of all people know how important relaxation is for a person's mental health."

"You're playing dirty." Cody laughed. "Okay. What can I bring?"

"Nothing. You're a guest. We'll even have towels if you decide to go swimming at the island."

"Fine—" The ping of Cody's cell phone interrupted the rest of his sentence. He withdrew it from his pocket and saw another text from his kid sister. *Where are you?* He looked at his friend. "I've got to take this."

"Everything all right?"

"Just my sister." Cody headed for the back door to step outside onto the gallery where it was quiet. His sister only texted him when she was having problems. The last one was her way of asking him to call her. Now.

Hannah answered on the first ring. "Am I glad you called!"

"What's wrong?"

"Everything. Where are you? I thought you would be at your apartment."

"At my apartment? Where are you?"

"Outside your door, getting funny looks from your neighbors."

Chapter Two

"What do you mean you're outside my door? You're here in Hope?" Cody's hand tightened around his cell. Hannah had never done something like this. They'd talked over the phone and worked out her problems.

"Yes, I'm here. What else would *standing outside your door* mean?" Hannah's exasperation matched his.

"I'll be there in about ten minutes."

"Hurry. The mosquitoes are feasting on me."

Cody went back inside to say good-night and found Maggie standing with her uncle, Ruth and Kim near the cake table.

Maggie smiled as he came up to them. "Do you want a slice?"

"Can't. I have to leave and wanted to thank you all for the invite."

"Is everything all right?" Ruth Sommerfield asked, taking hold of her husband's arm.

"My sister has shown up at my apartment without telling me she was coming."

"Where does she live?" Kim turned toward the table and cut two slices of the cake.

"Los Angeles."

Keith whistled. "She came a fair piece to see you, and you didn't know about it?"

"No. That's my sister."

Kim handed him the paper plate with the cake on it. "Take this and enjoy it. Both of you."

Cody smiled his thanks. "Hannah has a sweet tooth. She'll appreciate this. Good night and congratulations again, Keith and Ruth."

"I'll walk you out," Maggie said and fell into step beside him.

"You don't need to do that."

"No, I don't, but I want to." She peered over her shoulder as they walked toward the staircase leading down to the first floor of the antebellum house. "It's so nice not to have large sheets of plastic cordoning off the areas that needed renovating. It's looking more and more like home again."

"That's so much a part of the problem with disasters. Seeing the effects for months later. Rebuilding takes time but sometimes people need immediate results or depression sets in."

"I know that was part of Uncle Keith's problem. I've seen it with so many others. There are still people who are homeless, a lot thankfully living in trailers they received from the government."

"But it isn't the same. They don't look at the trailer as their home."

"Then we could get into a discussion about what makes a home."

He grinned. "We better avoid that this time. My sister is expecting me this evening." He didn't think his definition would be what Maggie's was. She saw it as a physical place; he thought of it as a mental one.

"You're right. Home means different things to different people." Maggie stopped at the front entrance. "I wanted to thank you again for helping me on the elevator and understanding about me freaking out."

"I've seen it before. It takes a lot more than that to get to me."

"I'm glad to hear that. Good night."

Cody left Bienville, his steps light, thanks to Maggie's warm smile. It hadn't been a bad evening after all, especially out in the garden. At times like that, when he was with someone intriguing like Maggie, he wanted to reconsider his plans. But he was doing what he was supposed to. He couldn't turn his back on the people he helped. Still, thoughts of Maggie stayed with him until he pulled into the parking space in front of his apartment and saw his sister on his doorstep.

Pregnant.

Maggie leaned against one of the opened double doors after Cody drove away. Sounds of the party—laughter and voices—floated down to her, but she wasn't in any hurry to return. The smile Cody gave her when he had left caused flutters in her stomach like the wings of the hummingbirds that visited her garden every day.

She sighed. Too bad he would be leaving Hope in a few months. It would be interesting to get to know him better.

She shut the door and ascended the staircase to the second floor. But instead of rejoining the party, she went to look for her son. She hadn't seen Brady for a while. Was he in his room?

Maggie made a detour toward her son's bedroom. When he said, "Come in," she found him on his bed, staring up at the ceiling.

"You okay?"

With his gaze still fixed on a spot above him, he murmured, "Yeah."

But the way he said that one word told her he was far from all right. "What happened?"

Finally Brady looked at her. "Nothin'. I'm tired."

She crossed to his bed and sat. "Hon, you've been tired a lot lately. Sleeping all the time. Are you feeling okay?"

"Mom! Don't get on my case about sleeping. It's not like I'm out doing anything I shouldn't." He rolled away from her.

"After church tomorrow we're going to Nathan's. He needs help painting the last few rooms in his house. He'll finally be through with all the repairs after Hurricane Naomi. I'm sure there will be time for you to ride Jersey."

"I don't wanna go."

"You don't?" This was a first. He always loved going to his cousin's farm just north of Hope, especially riding the gelding. He even tolerated Carly, Nathan's daughter, following him around even though she was only six years old.

"I said I didn't."

"Has something happened?"

He didn't say anything.

"Brady, what's wrong?"

He turned back to her. "What's wrong is that you keep asking me that. I'm fine. I just want to be left alone."

Having her son lash out at her hurt. They had

always been so close until the past few months. Was this what it was like to have a teenage boy? She really didn't have anyone to talk to about this. Uncle Keith had already told her that, when he was a teenager, life had been different.

Brady turned on his side away from her. "I'm tired, Mom. Good night."

She started to say, "But it's only nine o'clock." Biting her bottom lip, she rose and left the room.

Something was wrong. Yes, it could be Brady's age, but she didn't really think that was it. He usually spent most of his free time with his best friends, Adam and Jesse, but lately he wasn't doing that. More and more she would find him here in his room, alone. Scrubbing her hands down her face, she wished she had a man to turn to. Being a single mom was getting harder and harder. Her son needed a father. And his was dead. Killed in action while serving his country.

Thirteen years ago she'd been marking off the days on the calendar for when her fiancé, Robbie, would return from serving overseas and they could finally marry. His unit had been deployed unexpectedly to reinforce a troubled area off the coast of Africa. They hadn't wanted to elope or have a quickie marriage, so they were going to wait until he came home. In the meantime, she had been planning the wedding—a wedding that never occurred. Instead, she went to a funeral. Only a couple weeks after that, she discovered she was pregnant.

Pregnant and mourning the death of her fiancé had left her devastated and full of anger. She'd made some mistakes, but later, as she'd learned when she'd become a Christian, God didn't care. He loved her no matter what. It was Kim who had insisted Maggie go to church with her a couple Sundays after Maggie had discovered she was going to have Robbie's child. That had been the beginning. As she'd learned to be a Christian, she'd learned to be a mother, too, with a lot of trials and errors because her mother had never been a good role model.

If it hadn't been for the Lord, she would have fallen apart when her mother had turned her back on her, embarrassed that she was going to have a baby out of wedlock and even worse, she was going to keep her child. In the depth of Maggie's despair, God's words reached her. When Brady had been born, she welcomed him into this world as part of Robbie that lived on. She vowed she would do what she could to love and protect their son.

Now something wasn't right, and she didn't know what to do. *Lord, I need You. What's going on with Brady? You've always been here for me. Help me again now.*

"Who's the father, Hannah?" Cody paced from one end of his living room to the other.

"Aaron, of course."

"Then why did he leave you?"

"He told me he didn't want to be a father, packed his bags and walked out the door. He left me to pay the rent. I couldn't afford it by myself. I didn't know what else to do so I came to see you. I'm broke. Seeing the doctor took all my money. I want to do what's best for the baby, but I don't even have enough to see the doctor again." His twenty-two-year-old sister rattled off her reply, barely taking a breath between sentences. Standing by the kitchen bar that opened into the living room, she clutched one of the tall stools with her left hand while the right rubbed her large stomach.

"How many months are you? Eight? Why didn't you tell me this before now?"

"I'm almost five months."

"Are you sure?" She looked much farther along than that, but then he wasn't an expert on pregnant women.

"Yes, as sure as you can be." Her gaze dropped to the floor. "I was hoping Aaron would want to get married before the baby came. Instead he ran away as fast as he could."

"When did that happen?"

She lifted her face, tears glistening in her eyes. "Two months ago. I knew how disappointed you would be with me. I was trying to make a go of it alone. But I can't." Tears ran down her cheeks. "I'm a failure and I don't know what to do."

He came to her and drew her into his arms, her sobs punching a hole in his heart. "I'll help. You know I will. You're all the family I have." As he said those words in the calmest voice he could muster, panic zipped through him. He could counsel others, but he'd always had a hard time with his little sister. When their parents died, first their mother then five years later their father, Hannah had turned more and more to him. And the one time she should have come to him right away, she hadn't.

"I let you down." She tightened her hold on him.

As he stroked her back, trying to give her all the support he could, he listened to her sobs. *What do I do, Lord?* Suddenly all those times he'd helped others didn't mean anything if he couldn't help his own sister.

Finally she pulled away, wiping her tears from her cheeks. "All I do anymore is cry. I'm big as a house. I guess that's what happens when you're gonna have twins."

Cody felt the color drain from his face as he stared at Hannah. "Twins?" Maybe he hadn't heard correctly.

"Yeah, what did you think? I look like I'm seven or eight months along."

Cody sank onto his couch, his head ringing as though he'd been a punching bag for a boxer. "Is that why Aaron left?"

"No, I didn't even get a chance to tell him that. When he heard I was going to have a baby, he hung up on me."

"You told him that news over the phone?"

"Yeah, I was upset. I thought I had indigestion or heartburn or both. Then when I went to the doctor and found out I was going to have a baby, I had to talk to him right away. I can't do this alone. I can't."

"You're not alone. I'll think of something." But the panic that had gripped him earlier still had a firm hold on him. He was so out of his element.

"Do I hafta go?" Brady asked for the second time as he lugged the cooler of food down the pier early the Fourth of July morning. "I can walk home from here."

"And what are you gonna do when you get there?" Maggie stepped onto Zane's sixty-foot boat.

Her son shrugged. "Nothin'."

"You can do nothing here and maybe, just maybe, you'll have some fun."

Brady frowned and passed the cooler to her, then hopped onto the deck. "You can't make someone have fun."

"Sure I can." She forced a smile to her lips. "Your mother has spoken."

He looked at her as though she were crazy and stomped into the cabin.

"Not a bad technique. I'm gonna have to try that with Anna," Kim said as she came aboard the *Blue Runner*.

"You wait. Anna only has a few more years and then she'll be a teenager."

"Technically Brady isn't one for a few weeks."

"Tell that to his raging hormones. At least I hope that's what it is. Otherwise, I don't know what to do."

"And you know what to do about raging hormones?"

"Good point."

"I'm sure that's all it is. I wish some parent would come up with a way our kids can skip the teenage years."

Maggie scanned the dock. "Where's Zane and Anna?"

"They're coming with half the kitchen."

"Who else is coming?"

"Well, Dad and Ruth—"

Maggie's gaze strayed to the end of the pier. "Ah, I see them with—Cody. I didn't realize Zane had asked him." She'd glimpsed him a couple of times at City Hall earlier in the week but hadn't had a chance to say anything to him. She'd noticed he looked tired and wondered why. His job should be getting easier as people put their lives back together.

Kim's voice broke into her thoughts. "Zane and Cody need to talk about the housing project, and they are both so busy they decided to combine business and pleasure. They don't know I'm declaring a day of no work."

Maggie chuckled. "Oh, this will be entertaining."

"Anna wants to deep-sea fish."

"Who's that woman with Cody? His sister?" She didn't like how her stomach clenched at the sight of the beautiful blonde who could be no more than twenty-three. Surely it was his sister.

"Yes. She came to stay with him, so naturally Zane invited her, too."

The young woman moved the bag she was carrying, and Maggie saw her rounded stomach. "She's pregnant."

"Yes, and that's all I know. Cody hasn't said much about why she's here. He wasn't going to join us today because of her, but Zane talked him into it." Kim mounted the steps to the enclosed cabin, taking her straw purse and stack of towels inside.

Maggie peered from brother to sister. Other than the blue eyes, they didn't look like family. But then her younger brother didn't look anything like her. Or at least he hadn't ten years ago when he'd left Hope to see the world not long after her parents had retired in Sedona. Occasionally she'd get an email from Eli, letting her know he was still alive but not much more than that. She wished Brady had a chance to know his uncle Eli. But to her brother, family didn't mean much.

When Cody boarded the *Blue Runner,* his gaze caught Maggie's. A smile reached his eyes, then he murmured something to his sister who glanced at Maggie. The heat of a blush touched her cheeks. What had he said? And why did she care?

Maggie shifted around to help Zane with the provisions, taking a box from him and heading for the cabin. As she balanced the box on her hip to open the door, Cody scooted around her and pushed it open.

"Thanks." Warmth still blazed her cheeks as she entered the cabin. Inside she found Kim as she placed the box on the counter. "Did you clean out your kitchen or something?"

"Or something," Kim said as she brought out doughnuts.

Maggie plucked one up, her mouth watering at the delight she was about to enjoy. "The best doughnuts on the Gulf Coast are from Rhonda's Bakery." She took a bite. "Mmm."

"You're drooling," Cody whispered close to her ear and reached around her to snatch a doughnut. "I can't let you do it alone."

She watched him bring Rhonda's signature pastry to his lips.

He sank his teeth into the sweet treat, his eyes closing. "I'm going to miss this when I leave."

The reminder of Hope being only a temporary stop for Cody sobered Maggie. She quickly began shoring up her defenses. *He's just a friend. No, an acquaintance only. Remember that.* Too many people she'd loved in her life had left her—Robbie, her parents and her brother. "That's one of many things this town has to offer." She swiveled around and went back outside to see if there was anything else she could bring into the cabin.

Don't get involved. I've got everything I need here. I've been through one life-changing relationship that left me brokenhearted. That's enough.

Chapter Three

Cody didn't have to be versed in reading people's emotions to know that Maggie was upset about something. Since he was a young child, he'd learned to read others while keeping himself emotionally closed off. That was the only way he could survive moving from one place to another all the time, like early on when he had had to say goodbye to his best friend, a boy who lived two houses down from him on base. They had liked the same things and they had played for hours every day. But he had to move. Before long he'd learned to cultivate lots of casual friends but never one who it would hurt to leave.

"What did you say to her?" Hannah asked him as she eased down on a seat in the air-conditioned cabin.

"How much I love Rhonda's doughnuts." He

lifted his shoulder in a shrug, not sure what else he'd said.

Hannah tried one of the sweets. "Oh, these are good. Too good. I may be eating for three, but I still have to watch what kinds of foods I eat."

Kim opened a carton of orange juice and poured some into a paper cup. "I'm glad we only do this occasionally. These are like potato chips. I can't just eat one." Taking a doughnut, she slid in next to Hannah on the padded bench.

With his sister occupied talking with Kim, Cody slipped outside just as Zane and Keith untied the ropes from the piling. He found Maggie sitting in one of the fishing chairs. Sunglasses perched on his nose, Cody went to stand against the railing near her.

As Zane eased the *Blue Runner* out of its slip at the pier, Cody looked at Maggie. The breeze picked up strands of her long hair and whipped them in the air about her face. "Zane said something about going deep-sea fishing first."

She swung her head toward him, her dark brown eyes hidden by her sunglasses. "Brady loves to go fishing. I'm hoping he'll get into it today."

"He didn't want to be here?"

"No, I had to practically drag him out of bed this morning."

"Up late?"

"No, he went to sleep early last night. I hope he isn't coming down with something. He's been sleeping a lot lately whereas I," one corner of her mouth lifted up, "have only gotten about half of what he has. Is it possible to borrow hours from another?"

"When you figure out how, let me know."

"You're having trouble, too?"

"Yeah, since Hannah showed up on my doorstep."

"Is there a problem? You haven't talked much about your sister. In fact, until the other day, I didn't even know you had one."

Taking the chair next to Maggie, Cody glanced toward the cabin and spied Hannah laughing at something Keith had said to her. "She's pregnant and on her own."

"Oh."

Although he couldn't see Maggie's eyes, he felt the walls going up between them. He hastened to say, "I'll support her any way I can. But the problem is I don't know exactly what to do for Hannah."

The tense set to Maggie's shoulders relaxed. "Be there for her. She'll need it. Is the father out of the picture totally?"

"It sounds like it. The minute he realized she was pregnant he left her."

"Leaving her to handle it by herself. How chivalrous of him."

"Aaron's armor was definitely rusted."

"Were they planning on getting married?"

"In Hannah's mind, yes. I doubt it ever crossed Aaron's."

"If she needs someone to talk to, I've been through what's happening to her. I'll be glad to talk to her."

"Brady's father left you?"

"We were planning to get married until he was deployed earlier than he was supposed to be. He was killed in action." A defensive tone sounded in her voice.

"I'm sorry to hear that. That had to be hard on you."

"Brady needs a father. A mother isn't the same thing, especially right now. Uncle Keith has helped, but I can see that he doesn't always understand what Brady is going through. Growing up fifty years ago is a lot different from growing up today. Kids have challenges he didn't have back then."

Early on Cody had discovered the key to getting to know someone was to let them talk and to listen. It had certainly helped him in his job.

"Yeah, kids back then were less likely to face challenges like drugs and being bombarded with sex and violence everywhere they go. Also, kids today want instant gratification. When you can press a button and change the channel in less than a second, waiting around for even a slow computer to load can be exasperating to them."

"Actually to me, too." Her laugh sprinkled the air with her merriment. "We have been spoiled by everything becoming faster and faster."

"Life is flying past us." It wasn't that long ago his sister had been in high school and living with him. Now she would be a mother.

"That's what my boss keeps saying to me. I need to slow down and actually taste the food I cook. I told Ruth she needed to give me an hour for lunch. And she did. Now I don't have an excuse for wolfing down my food. Except it's a habit."

The overhang from the top deck threw the stern into the shade. Maggie took off her sunglasses, removing a barrier between them. Cody did likewise, feeling a subtle change in their relationship.

"I confess a habit I can't break is rushing out the front door without eating breakfast. I pick up coffee on the way to work. That's it until lunch.

Except for that doughnut this morning. I just can't get myself up and going as quickly as I should."

"When you have children, they will cure you of that."

His lifestyle wasn't conducive to having children. Some of the places he was sent to were struggling and primitive. He wouldn't want to raise a baby in that kind of environment. So what was he going to do about his sister?

"Hannah is going to have twins."

Maggie whistled. "All her problems will be doubled. How about making the father financially support his children?"

Cody shook his head. "She doesn't want to have anything to do with him. If he doesn't want his children, then she'll make it somehow. Of course, she doesn't have insurance or a job."

"What does she do?"

"She's an electrician."

Maggie's eyes widened. "Look on the bright side. This is a good place to come. We're in need of electricians. She needs to talk with Zane. He's expanding again—forming another crew."

"Have you taken a close look at her? She's not even five months pregnant yet, but she looks much more than that. It won't be long before she'll have problems performing that job."

She reached out and clasped his lower arm.

"I'll help. I grew up with Zane. He's a problem solver, and he'll have a solution. And I meant it when I said I can talk to her. I'm willing to help her any way I can. Someone helped me. I want to return the favor."

"Having you as a friend will be a good start for Hannah in Hope." Maybe then he'd be able to leave her and feel all right with it when the time came. He didn't want to drag Hannah and her kids around the world. He was used to it, but she'd made an effort to put down roots when she had turned eighteen and declared she didn't like moving. Yet, that didn't feel right to him. Hannah was his only family.

"Good. Consider it done. After we fish, we'll have some downtime on the island to picnic and swim. I'll talk to her then and get things started."

Rising, she slipped on her sunglasses. "If you want any more doughnuts, you'd better stake your claim now. Uncle Keith keeps coming back to the counter and grabbing more. I've seen him eat half a dozen in no time."

"I will," he said as she started for the cabin door. He wished she hadn't put on her sunglasses. He enjoyed watching her emotions dance in her eyes.

Anna giggled as she reeled in a wiggling red snapper. "We'll get to eat it tonight."

"Probably not tonight because of the Fourth of July picnic at Broussard Park." Standing at the side of the boat, Maggie leaned over and grabbed the line to bring the catch onto the deck. "This is a big one."

The little girl stuck the rod in the holder in the chair and clapped her hands.

Maggie loved hearing her cousin's enthusiasm. Her gaze strayed to her son, slouched in his seat, barely holding his pole. Brady hadn't even wanted to fish, but finally agreed more because she had encouraged him than because he desired to. Next time she wouldn't. If he did catch something, the rod would probably fly out of his hands and end up in the sea.

Zane bent over the railing above. "Is that enough? Are y'all ready to go to the island and eat lunch?"

"Yes." Anna pumped her arm in the air. "I'm starved."

Not a word from Brady. He did sit up straight and reel in his line. Maggie put the red snapper into the large cooler with the others they'd caught that morning. Making her way into the cabin, she washed her hands, the scent of fish wafting to her. She wrinkled her nose and scrubbed her skin. She hated that smell. It was Uncle Keith who had instilled the love of fishing in her son, not her.

When she finished, Cody passed her a paper towel. "I haven't been fishing in years. It was fun, but don't tell anyone I caught the smallest one."

"Not a word. But I can't guarantee Anna won't spread the word she brought in the biggest fish."

One corner of his mouth hiked up. "You're relishing this, aren't you?"

"Yep. My bonito was the second biggest." She shined her fingernails against her T-shirt.

He nodded toward the back. "I thought Brady loved to fish."

"He does—did. I guess he's still pouting because I made him come today. Which is a first. Usually he's out in the car waiting to go fishing."

"So what's changed lately?"

"Maybe he's bored because it's summer and hot. But that's never been a problem in the past."

"How was he after the hurricane? I've dealt with kids who've had problems in Hope."

"He seemed okay afterward. He helped where he could. You think this could be because of the storm? It was eight months ago."

"Some people have suppressed their fears, but eventually they come out. For many, the hurricane made them realize how temporary everything is. That's scary, especially for children. I can talk to him if you want."

"Several weeks ago I suggested he talk with our pastor. He got so angry at me. Said he was fine and stormed off. He didn't come out of his room the rest of the day, even for dinner. Which is *most* unusual."

"We could do it in a more casual way."

"Like what Kim had you do for Keith at the beginning before he acknowledged he had a problem?"

"Yes."

"It probably wouldn't work because Brady knows what Kim did."

"I'm around the family now socially some. We could make it more and see if that will break down any barriers."

"Do more of what we're doing today?" The prospects of seeing Cody more revved her heartbeat to a faster tempo.

"Yes. Sometimes that can be the best way to go."

"Isn't that more time-consuming?" She would be spending extra time with Cody. That was certainly not a bad thing. But then she remembered their talk earlier. Although he wore sunglasses and she couldn't read much in his expression, when he took them off later, he was still closed off to her. She had a feeling he didn't share much of himself with others. Was that because he had to listen to so many people's problems?

"Yes, but if it'll help, I don't mind. You're going to help me with my sister, so why shouldn't I return the favor?"

"Ah, I scratch your back and you scratch mine." Her disappointment crept into her voice. A friend helping a friend. Why did that bother her? She knew anything with Cody wouldn't go anywhere. Their goals were too different. She hated change. His life was a constant series of changes.

"Brady will require subtlety," she warned. "It sounds like we're planning a campaign."

"Sometimes when a person is reluctant to get help, you have to go at it in a different way. But also I want you to have his doctor examine him to make sure there isn't a physical cause behind this behavior change," Cody said.

"Good suggestion. I will."

The cabin door opened, and Brady entered and plopped into a seat next to Ruth. His frown and hunched shoulders attested to his mood and invaded the upbeat atmosphere. The light teasing from Anna and Kim stopped. Quiet fell over the group.

Uncle Keith came inside. "Zane said we're almost there and to pack up everything we want to take on the island."

No one moved right away.

Uncle Keith glanced from one to the other, waving his hand. "Let's hop to it. Cody, you can help me tie the boat to the pier. Brady, you're in charge of the chairs. Anna, you can take the two umbrellas for the shade lovers. Kim and Maggie, the food. We can't forget that." His gaze paused on his bride, and he smiled. "Ruth, you and Hannah can bring the towels, sunscreen and anything else you can think of."

"Dad is back to one hundred percent, giving orders like he used to." Kim rose and began gathering the supplies.

"I better get moving. I've got my marching orders." Cody started past Maggie.

She clasped his arm. "I think your plan is the only one that has a chance of working at the moment. I'm in."

He bent toward her and whispered, "Hopefully I'll be able to establish a connection with him. Even in a formal counseling session that's important." His hand cupped hers still on his arm.

She hadn't realize she was still touching him. Slipping her hand away, she said, "I hope so, too. Maybe we can plan something with both Brady and Hannah. Let me think on it. Maybe something after the Ultimate Garage Sale. I figure we'll all be attending."

"I hear you're a great cook. Anytime you want to cook for us will be appreciated."

Her pulse pounding through her body, she stepped back. "I'll take that under consideration. I made the potato salad and the fried chicken today. Also, I baked the bars that taste like pecan pie. Not as messy as cutting a pie." He hadn't needed a list of what she had cooked, but she couldn't think of anything else to say. He rattled her.

"I'm glad we're eating lunch before swimming. That doughnut wasn't nearly enough to satisfy my hunger pangs." He smiled at her before making his way toward the back to help dock the boat.

"See, now you understand why having a good breakfast is so important," Maggie called. "If you do, you aren't ravenous before noon."

Maggie watched him a moment, then realized she was staring at Cody. She averted her gaze but discovered that Kim was studying her from across the cabin. Her cousin raised her eyebrows, a smirk on her face. Oh, great. She'd never hear the end of it now.

Kim was out to fix up all single people in Hope. Maggie swung her attention to Ruth and caught her looking at her, too. Matchmaking was contagious obviously. Double whammy. She could see the wheels turning in both women's minds. It might be a long afternoon.

"So what were you and Cody talking about in the cabin earlier?" Kim splashed through the shallow water on the south side of the island in a protected cove where the waves were smaller than the other areas on the beach.

Dressed in a floppy hat that shaded her face, Maggie watched the guys clean up after lunch as Ruth and Anna built a sand castle while she and Kim walked along the beach. "If I tell you something, you need to keep it quiet. I don't want Brady to know what I've asked Cody to do—or rather what he's volunteered to do."

"He's going to counsel Brady without him knowing. Like Dad."

"Your father figured it out pretty fast, so he's going to be much more subtle with Brady. It's not like he doesn't know the family now."

"But still your son could suspect something." Kim moved out farther from shore, the water lapping the tops of her thighs. Her gaze fixed on Brady on shore, she tilted her head to the side. "So what are you gonna do?"

"I don't know. Convince Brady he needs help.

Cody wants me to talk to Hannah since I know what it's like to be alone and pregnant. Maybe by throwing us together, it'll evolve naturally."

"I hope it works. I've noticed how depressed Brady has been lately. I've been worried about him. Does Cody think it's being a teenager or something else?"

Maggie glanced over her shoulder at the others about a hundred feet away. "We just talked about it this morning. Cody's good but let's give him time. He did mention that some people have had delayed reactions to Hurricane Naomi, so I guess it could be that."

Kim planted her hand on her waist. "I didn't think of that. It could be. Right after it happened he was extra quiet like he is now. But then he began pitching in and was almost back to normal, so I dismissed those thoughts, especially when Dad went downhill."

"And Brady did a lot to help Uncle Keith. This new behavior didn't really appear until after your dad got better. To be on the safe side, I'm going to call his doctor tomorrow and have him check out Brady in case there's a physical reason he's so tired lately." From the corner of Maggie's eye, she glimpsed her son walking back toward the pier on the north side of the island. Anger marred his features. "I'd better go see what's going on."

Maggie exited the water and hotfooted it across the sand, the bottoms of her feet burning. After snatching up her flip-flops, she put them on as she hurried to catch Brady before he retreated from the family.

"Hon, where are you going?"

Brady slowed his pace but kept trudging along the worn path they used to traverse from one side of Eagle Island to the other side. "Going to the *Blue Runner.* Where else would I go? Back home where I want to be?"

Patience, Maggie. But it was wearing thin. "I'd like you to stay with us."

"I want to take a nap."

"But you already slept ten hours today."

"I'm tired. I must need more sleep."

"Then take a nap," she said, gesturing toward the beach where they had set up umbrellas, towels and chairs, "but do it here. This is not debatable. And next week I'm calling your doctor to get you a checkup. You've been tired a lot lately."

"I'm fine. Can't a guy sleep when he wants? It's summer. Summer is for resting."

"You're gonna have to humor me on this."

Scowling, Brady folded his arms over his chest.

When Maggie started her trek back to the beach, she paused after a few steps and waited for her son to catch up with her.

Anna squealed and began pointing to an area not far from where she was in the water.

Close to Anna, Cody sloshed through the Gulf to the girl and stared at what she indicated, then lifted his head and shouted, "It's a shark."

Chapter Four

"A shark?" Brady ran past Maggie as he headed toward the Gulf.

"Wait! Brady, you can't go in. It's a shark." Maggie hurried to catch up with him, visions of some of the sharks she'd seen caught off the Mississippi coast flashing through her mind. The last one was an eight-foot nurse shark with rows of sharp teeth.

Her son barely paused in his trek out into the sea. "It can't be too bad. Anna isn't running screaming out of the water."

Maggie swung her gaze to the pair still in the same spot. Anna jumped up and down, pointing. Cody stood calmly near her. Cupping her hands around her mouth, Maggie shouted, "How big is it?"

Looking toward her, Cody indicated about two-and-a-half feet.

Relief shivered down her until she remembered baby sharks still had teeth. Behind her son, she waded toward Cody and Anna about twenty yards offshore. On the beach Kim and Zane were walking toward the middle of the island and probably didn't hear Cody, but Ruth and Uncle Keith came to the edge of the water and watched.

"What's it doing?" Maggie asked as she approached the trio now observing the shark's movements.

"Just swimming in circles. Maybe it's looking for its mother." Anna glanced around.

"Cool." Her son's expression became excited, his attention glued to the shark.

"Probably it's searching for food smaller than us," Cody said with not an ounce of fear in his expression.

"Really?" Maggie checked where the predator was in relationship to her son—a few yards away.

"Yeah, Mom. Cody is probably right. We're safe. It sees us as a threat."

Anna screamed. "Look. I see a fin out there. Its mother is coming." The child backed up a few steps, her arm waving in the air.

Maggie followed the direction Anna indicated and saw a fin heading toward them about twenty yards away. "Let's get to shore. That's no thirty-inch shark."

Before she finished what she said, Cody had grabbed Anna's hand and started for the beach. Maggie did the same with Brady.

"Ah, Mom. It could be a dolphin." He shook off her grasp, but he kept going toward shore.

"Yeah, it could be, but it could be a shark. I'd rather not take the chance." Maggie threw a glanced over her shoulder and found the fin turning. The shark or whatever it was began swimming parallel to the beach but away from them. Drawing in a deep breath, she kept that information to herself in case Brady decided to turn around and head back out.

Once ashore, Anna ran up to her grandfather and Ruth, jumped around pointing at the larger fin in the water. "Papa Keith, what do you think that is? A dolphin or a shark?"

"It isn't swimming like a dolphin. It's gotta be a shark. Probably a reef one."

Brady joined them. "You think so? They can grow to be big."

"Yep. I saw one that was at least a foot longer than me." Uncle Keith rocked back on his heels in the sand.

Anna's eyes grew round. "While you were swimming?"

"Yes. I didn't panic, but I did get out of there."

"I'm sure you did, dear. I didn't marry a thrill

junkie, thank goodness." Ruth clasped Uncle Keith's hand.

He started back toward the umbrellas and chairs. "Oh, I don't know about that. Wait till you see what I have planned for our first-month anniversary."

"We'll celebrating month anniversaries?"

"When you get to be over sixty, I think it makes sense." Her uncle winked at Ruth. "Besides, celebrations are fun." He leaned close to his bride's ear and whispered something to her.

She giggled and playfully punched him in the arm.

"C'mon, Brady. Let's follow the shark down the beach." Anna started running.

Brady went after her.

"Don't go into the water," Maggie shouted, then slanted a look at Cody. "Did he hear me?"

"I think they heard you back in town."

"Just wanna make sure Brady heard me."

"Oh, he did."

The grin that spread across his face warmed her more than the sun beating down upon her. "One good thing about spotting the shark, Brady has forgotten about taking a nap."

Cody peered down the beach to where Anna and Brady were still jogging. "Good. He's still interested in some things."

"So all I have to do is get a pet shark for him. I don't think there's an aquarium big enough to hold a shark, even a baby one."

"I always wanted a cool pet while growing up."

"And you didn't have one? What did you have? A dog or cat?"

"Nothing."

"Not one animal?" The thought of him not having a pet saddened her. Brady loved animals. When he lost his dog right before the hurricane, she had intended to get him another one, but so much of her energy went into cleaning up Bienville and trying to get it back to the way it was, to taking care of her uncle, to helping others get some normalcy back.

"Nope, the closest I came to having one was when a guy in my class was going out of town and I babysat his dog for him."

Maggie noticed the kids trotting back toward them. "How old were you?"

"Ten, and I took my job very seriously. I had a ball for that week. I took his beagle to the park, played Frisbee with him and took him on hikes."

"Why didn't you get a pet? Just because you didn't stay put in a place doesn't mean you can't have pets."

"Not according to my dad, but then I really

think it was because Mom was allergic to dog and cat hair."

"There's always a fish or snake."

"What's cool about a fish unless it's a shark? And my mom banned snakes and rodents from the house."

"What's stopping you now?" Maggie asked as her son skirted around them and settled under an umbrella on a towel. Brady's enthusiasm had lasted about fifteen minutes.

"My job." Cody peered toward where she was staring. "We'll figure something out. There may be a time you'll have to tell him he needs to get some counseling."

"I know," she said on a long breath. "But like the saying, you can lead a horse to water, but you can't make him drink. That may be Brady."

"We'll cross that bridge when we come to it."

Maggie chuckled. "What is this? Cliché day?"

"If the shoe fits…" He shrugged.

In the midst of all her worrying, Maggie burst out laughing.

"Did I tickle your funny bone?"

"Uncle!"

As he laughed, Cody peered toward the others on the beach. "We're getting stares."

"Yeah." All except her son who had closed his eyes and was probably asleep. "All this talk about pets makes me realize I should get Brady another dog. His dog died a week before the hurricane. Frisky was fifteen. She had to be put down. That was hard for me and Brady, but it was way worse seeing her suffer."

"Brady didn't say anything after the hurricane?"

Maggie thought back to that time when their emotions were on overload, their energy sapped from working so much just to make the house livable. "I remember him saying something a couple times. I intended to see about a new pet, but then something else came up. When Uncle Keith got so bad, Brady stopped asking. He was sharing a bedroom with his great uncle and trying to help him as much as possible. With school, the house and Uncle Keith, there was little time left over."

"I would talk to him about it. Pets are great to help people who are depressed or floundering."

"Then I know the perfect place to take Brady to get the pet of his choice."

"Are you sure you want to give him a choice? Remember the shark."

"My cousin Nathan thankfully doesn't have sharks at his farm, but he does have an array of animals that Brady can choose from."

"Nathan Grayson?"

"Yeah. Do you know him?"

"We've gotten to know each other. I've sent several of my clients out to his farm to get a pet."

"Have you ever been out there?"

"No, I just know him from church."

"You need to go."

"I know. I've been meaning to."

"We're gonna help him finish painting the last few rooms in his house this Saturday. It took quite a beating during the storm. He's finally repaired the damage in between taking in abandoned animals and running his veterinary practice." Maggie swung her attention to her son still sleeping under the umbrella or at least pretending to. There was no way she could sleep through the noises the others were making—laughing and talking only feet away. "Brady's giving me a hard time about going. He's always loved going before, but lately it's been hard getting him to do anything. Now that he has his own room again, he has camped out in it. In past summers, I hardly saw him. He'd be gone from right after breakfast to right before dinner, playing with friends."

"Maybe he'll change his mind if he knows he gets to pick out a pet."

"True. I'm not above using a bribe—or should I say incentive. Can you come, too? The more help, the faster we get done, then we can enjoy the animals." She grinned. "Who knows? You might find a pet for yourself."

"Can I bring Hannah?"

"Oh, I like how you think. We could use someone to tape off the areas to be painted. I'll check with Nathan, but I can't imagine him turning down free labor."

"Not the Nathan I've gotten to know."

He'd ignored her suggestion about looking for an animal for himself, but she'd heard the hint of regret in his voice when he'd been talking about why he'd never had a pet. "Be prepared for him to try to talk you into taking a pet."

"Thanks for the warning. I'll have to work on my refusal."

Behind the sunglasses she couldn't really read his expression, but his voice conveyed the same tone as earlier. "It doesn't have to be like that. You could become a foster owner until Nathan finds a more permanent home."

"I think I need to leave well enough alone. No sense getting attached."

But the regret still sounded in his voice. It touched Maggie in a place she kept hidden from the world. She had let Robbie into it, and the hurt had been unbearable when he was killed.

The heat of the Fourth of July still lingered although the sun started its descent behind the tall trees on the west part of Broussard Park. The scent of salt infused with the sweet smell of hon-eysuckle and jasmine drifted to Maggie on the light breeze blowing in from the sea and across the new garden the ladies of Hope Garden Club had planted last month. Sitting on the large daisy-print blanket, she watched people find a spot for their picnic dinner and an area to watch the fireworks right after dark.

She spied Cody and Hannah crossing the park and waved to let the pair know where they had settled for the evening. Cody smiled and hurried his pace. Maggie's heartbeat sped up. She tried to even out its beating, but the fact the man was staring right at her as though she were the only other person in the park sent a thrill through her.

"I had a hard time finding a parking space." Cody placed a store-bought dessert on the top of the cooler, then sat next to Hannah on the blanket right across from Maggie. "Where's Brady?"

"He's here. One of his friends persuaded him to play some basketball."

"That's good. And Zane?"

"With the boys, refereeing. Uncle Keith and Gideon are helping him." Gideon, Ruth's son-in-law, and his family—Kathleen, his wife, and her two sons by her first marriage—had joined them half an hour ago after Gideon got off work as a firefighter.

"Aah, maybe I should go see if he needs any

help." Cody rose in one fluid motion and walked toward the court on the other side of the park.

Hannah watched her brother leave. With a shake of her head, she swung her attention to Maggie. "How many adults does it take to referee?"

Maggie laughed. "Probably half the guys here." She nodded her head toward the court. "There's a group of men gathering. You know how they get when it comes to sports."

"I used to go to Cody's football games as a little girl. He enjoyed football and other kinds of sports, but it wasn't everything to him. My ex-boyfriend took the whole sports thing so seriously. I should have known he didn't really love me when going to a game with his buddies or watching one at home was more important than doing something with me."

"Is this the father of your babies?"

Hannah nodded, a sheen of tears in her eyes. "How can a man just walk away from his own children? Not even give them a chance?"

"I wish I had a good answer for that, but there isn't one. Brady's dad was killed in action and didn't have a chance to be a father. He died not even knowing he was going to be a father. I know he would have been a good one. He'd wanted children." The fallout from Robbie's death still affected her and Brady. Would her son have been able to relate better to Robbie about what was going on right now than he was with her?

"I'm sorry to hear that. I'm glad he at least wanted his kid."

"Yeah, but it didn't make things easy. I wasn't married. My mother was upset with me and let me know it. No, upset is too mild a word. Furious is more like it. I struggled to make ends meet. If it hadn't been for Uncle Keith stepping in and offering me a home, I don't know what I would have done. I didn't have any health insurance, and having a baby is expensive."

"I know what you mean. I'm young and working in a male-dominated field. I had only recently finished up my training when Aaron walked out on me so I don't have a lot of experience yet. Some employers where I lived were hesitant to hire a woman with next-to-no real experience. Then you add that I was pregnant, and the job I did have didn't last. There isn't any proof that was the reason I was let go, but when I began to show, things changed at the company where I worked." Hannah laid her hand on her rounded stomach. "It's getting a little hard to hide the fact that I'm pregnant. In a tight job market, people don't want to hire someone who is pregnant and will have to go on maternity leave shortly after they start."

Listening to Hannah speak of some of the problems she'd run into brought back all the pain and stress she'd gone through while grieving for the loss of Robbie. "I have a few connections here. Let me see what I can do. That is if you want to get a job here."

"I don't want to be a burden to Cody. Not that he has said anything to me about that. He never would. But I know he'll be moving on soon. He always does."

Hannah's statement rang in Maggie's ears. She remembered what Cody had said earlier about not wanting to foster a pet until Nathan could find a home for it. *No sense getting attached.* Was that his motto?

"I don't want to move if I can find a place where I can make a living and raise my children, but I don't think I can do it alone, especially having twins."

"That does make it more challenging. It's hard enough having one without support."

"I've always wanted to be a mother." One corner of Hannah's mouth tilted upward. "Not the way I did it and not at this time, but I don't have a choice now."

Maggie's heart twisted at the resignation she

heard in Hannah's word. She'd been there. She knew exactly what Cody's sister was going through. Reaching toward Hannah, Maggie covered the younger woman's hand. "I'll help anyway I can. You can call me anytime you think things are getting overwhelming. Or when you just need a friend to talk to. I know you have your brother right now, but sometimes it's nice to talk to a woman."

"But you don't know me. I can't impose on you."

"I know you more than you think. You're scared. You don't know which way to turn. Fear for the future dominates your thoughts. Does that about sum it up?"

"Exactly." The tears glistened in Hannah's eyes. She blinked, several tears rolled down her cheeks. "Cody is a wonderful brother, but there are some things I just can't talk to him about."

"Kim was and still is the person I go to when I need a woman to talk to. Although Uncle Keith was wonderful to me, like a second father, he couldn't understand the grief I was experiencing—not just the loss of Robbie, but of our dreams." But at least Keith had been there when Maggie's father had gone along with her mother and turned away from her. Oh, they'd talked a few times over the years, but nothing that could help them reconnect. "I can't imagine me talking to my brother about stuff like being pregnant, uncomfortable, feet swelling, even feeling the baby moving for the first time, that kick in the middle of the night that woke me up after finally getting to sleep."

"You have a brother?"

"Yeah, but he doesn't live here. He left and has been working in the far corners of the world on different construction projects."

"What's he do?"

"Structural engineering. He's smart, driven and busy."

"That's my brother."

Maggie laughed. "Yes, it does sound like him. We have a lot in common."

Shifting on the blanket, Hannah released a sigh. "I haven't even been here a week, and I'm already feeling welcomed as if I've come home."

"That's Hope for you. We're a little frazzled since the hurricane, but the town has always been welcoming to newcomers." Maggie leaned back, supporting herself with her arms. "I don't know about you, but I'm starved."

Kim joined them on the blanket. "Did I hear you're starved?"

"Yep, I think I'll go find the guys and tell them

we're eating whether they come or not. That oughta move them."

"It'll move my husband. Zane always looks forward to any food you cook."

Maggie pushed herself to her feet. "I knew there was a reason I liked him."

As Hannah and Kim chatted on the blanket, Maggie crossed half the park. She weaved in and out of groups of people until she came to the basketball court and squeezed through the crowd surrounding it. When she made her way to the front of the spectators, she came to a halt as Cody jumped up and caught the basketball.

Coming down right in front of her.

She quickly stepped back to avoid a collision. What happen to the refereeing? He sprinted into the center of the court and passed the ball to Brady who dribbled toward the basket, set his feet and took a shot. Cheers went up when he made it. Brady turned, a grin on his face, while Cody gave him a high five.

As Zane, a member of the other team, ran past her, she yelled above the noise, "We're going to eat."

He passed the ball to another teammate, then glanced toward her while guarding Cody. "We'll be there soon. We're about to beat these guys."

"Not if I have anything to say about it," Cody said, then dodged around Zane.

"That's fine. Come when you can. That is if there is any food left." She swiveled around on her heel and plunged back through the crowd watching the friendly rivalry. But she did throw one last look back at the court in time to see Cody steal the ball from Zane.

Out of the corner of his eye, Cody glimpsed Maggie disappear into the crowd right before he sent the ball to Brady nearer the basket. Another point and they would win. Brady weaved around a boy about his size and leaped up, releasing the ball. It went through the hoop.

"Yes!" Brady pumped his arm up and down. "We won."

Cody slapped him on the back. "You're good. I can't believe you didn't want to play. I'm glad you decided to."

"So am I." His grin spread across his face. "Did Mom say something about eating?"

"Yes. It's starting to get dark."

Zane approached. "And the fireworks will start in forty-five minutes." While the crowd dispersed, he swiped his hand across his forehead. "I hope you're going out for the team this year, Brady."

"Maybe."

Zane paused. "Maybe? You're a natural."

Cody noticed some of the excitement of the game was wearing off for Brady and he was beginning to retreat. "I have to agree, but with your quickness and size, football would be a good sport, too."

"Oh, yeah, you're right," Zane agreed. "How about it, Brady? I used to play for the Hope Mustangs."

Brady slowed his pace, his head dropping some. "Maybe. I don't know what I wanna do."

Zane exchanged a look with Cody.

He shook his head and said, "So what did your mom fix? That's all Zane has been talking about."

Brady lifted his gaze to Cody. "Her strawberry and blueberry cobbler with homemade vanilla ice cream. She makes the best."

"I can attest to that," Zane said. "I'm personally looking forward to the sandwiches she made out of a brisket she cooked last night. Drove my dad crazy while he was putting finishing touches to the living room. Dad has loved putting Bienville back the way it was. One more room and the house will be like before the storm."

Brady snorted and sped up.

Zane frowned. "Did I say something wrong?"

"Not really. Has anything changed for Brady as far as the house goes since the hurricane?"

"His room. With the fire a few months back, he had to move it."

"Aah, that might explain his actions. He doesn't see that everything is back to normal since Hurricane Naomi."

"Of course not. You and I both know that doesn't happen, not even years later. A disaster changes a place."

"And people." Cody observed Brady grab a sandwich and some chips then park himself off away from the rest of the family.

Cody sat down on the blanket between Hannah and Maggie. "Is there any food left?"

"Barely. Uncle Keith and Gideon nearly took it all." Maggie handed him a paper plate with a sandwich. "But the desserts are still intact."

"Zane says I have to try some of yours."

"It's your patriotic duty to try some."

"Patriotic?" Cody took a bite of his sandwich, the taste of the barbecue brisket delicious.

"It's red, white and blue. What else would you have on the Fourth of July?"

"You got me there. I picked up the only thing left at the grocery store on the way over here." There had been many Fourths of July while he'd been out of the country. It was nice this year to be here. Last year he'd been in an Asian country damaged by an earthquake that had left many homeless. "It's been a while since I've seen fireworks."

"I love them. The town shoots them right offshore."

Hannah leaned around her brother. "Mustang Island? How did it get its name?"

"In the 1800s at the time of the Civil War, some horses escaped their owner and swam to the island. A small herd lived there for many years."

"Do they now?"

"No. A hurricane at the turn of the century took what was left of the herd."

"How sad."

While Hannah and Maggie engaged in a conversation about the horses, Cody saw a connection growing between his sister and Maggie. Hannah, much like him, held herself back from most people, but not Maggie. She was so open it was hard to resist that in her.

By the time darkness fell and dinner was over, Cody lounged back on the blanket, his head cushioned by his crossed arms. He turned slightly toward Maggie next to him, her face beautiful in the soft glow from the parking lot lights a couple hundred feet away. "So this is the best way to watch the fireworks?"

She angled her head so he couldn't see her expression, but he felt her gaze on him. "The only way. Your neck won't get cramped. Since Mustang Island isn't far from shore, they'll go off practically on top of us."

The parking lot lights blinked off. Right after that, a boom filled the air, followed by a bright streak shooting up into the black sky. The fireworks opened up into a glittering shower of red, blue and silver. Cody glanced at Maggie and found her staring at him. The glow from the fireworks highlighted her face in a brilliance that captivated him. He missed the second one exploding above him because her gaze roped his full attention.

He inched closer to her and whispered, "Thank you for talking with Hannah."

"You're welcome. She reminds me of myself thirteen years ago."

"Sometimes it's hard to help someone you're close to."

"Yeah, I'm finding that out with Brady. I was glad to see him playing in the game with y'all earlier. He likes basketball, but he hasn't played much with his friends lately. How hard was it to get him to agree?"

"We needed one more kid. He took a look at the others and decided he would do it."

"Peer pressure. Sometimes it can work for the good."

"As most things, there's a good side and a bad

side to peer pressure. What's important is being able to teach our kids the difference between the two."

"You'll make a good father."

He stiffened at the implication of her statement. He'd had a good father who had tried to do his best. He wasn't often there for him and Hannah, but that happened when a man served his country and had a job that caused him to be gone a lot. Cody had learned to accept those times his father couldn't come to a football game, a school play or whatever he'd done as a child.

But until Maggie had made the comment, he hadn't really thought about being a father. With Beth the conversation had never come up. Did he really have what it took to be a father? He did know he wouldn't be one unless he could do more than his father. Good intentions weren't always enough for a child who needed a parent. He'd seen what happened when a parent neglected his child for work or something else. And right now he had dedicated himself to his work.

Chapter Five

Maggie pulled into the dirt road that led to Nathan's farm on the outskirts of Hope on the north side of Interstate 10. When it was quiet and the wind blew from the south, she could hear the traffic on the highway zooming toward New Orleans or Mobile.

"I'm here under protest." Brady folded his arms over his chest and stared out the side window. "I don't think I'm ready for another dog after Frisky."

"That's fine. No pressure here. We're mainly coming to help Nathan finish up. Bienville is almost back to normal. It'll be nice to help our cousins get their house fixed up, too."

Brady sighed so loudly the sound filled the whole interior of the car. "And I'm not riding even if Carly asks me to."

"Fine. We're probably not going to have time for it anyway."

"What are we gonna do? Work the whole time?"

"That's the point of today." Maggie made sure that Cody had made the right turn and was still following her car.

"It's Saturday."

"In the summer. Saturday isn't any different from the other days of the week for you."

Another big release of a loud breath.

"Brady Sommerfield, when have you not wanted to help others, especially in our family?"

"What if it's for nothing?"

"It won't be."

"How do you know? One day our home was there, and the next it was almost destroyed."

The anger-filled words hung in the air between them, reinforcing what Cody had said concerning her son's latest behavior, that Brady could be reacting to the hurricane, even months after the fact, especially now that hurricane season had started again.

"You're right. I don't know one hundred percent, but most likely it will be fine," Maggie said to his first outward comment concerning the hurricane in months.

"That's not good enough."

She parked in front of Nathan's brick one-story

ranch-style house. "That's all I can give you. Life is full of change. It's how we handle the change that's important. It's all we can control."

"Still not good enough." Brady shoved open his door and jumped from the car.

The slam of the door reverberated through the inside, underscoring her child's frame of mind. If she didn't see Cody coming toward her out of the side mirror, she would have banged her forehead against the steering wheel in frustration. Instead she gripped it so tightly pain zipped up both arms.

When Cody paused outside her vehicle, she exited it and leaned against its side. "Just in case you couldn't read his body language, Brady isn't happy about being here, even with the suggestion he could find a dog to take back to Bienville."

Cody glanced at his sister climbing from his car. "On the other hand, Hannah was downright thrilled she was getting out of the apartment. If she doesn't get a job soon, she and I will go crazy." His sister made her way to the porch and knocked on the door.

"Has she talked with Zane yet?"

"Monday. He was in New Orleans these past few days."

"I think that'll be a formality mostly. He was interested in the fact she's an electrician. He should be finished putting together this team he needs for a new project sometime next week."

"But what's she going to do when she can't work because of her pregnancy? That will be only a couple months away."

"Knowing Zane, he'll use her somewhere else until she can work again as an electrician. Quit worrying. Hope takes care of its own."

"But she isn't part of the town."

"She lives here, doesn't she?"

Cody cocked his head to the side and stared at her. "Yes, but…"

She placed her hand on his arm. "Quit worrying. That's an order."

One of his eyebrows rose. "An order?"

"Yep. Now let's go inside. Nathan is gonna wonder where we are."

The front door flew open, and Nathan's six-year-old daughter charged out onto the porch. "Maggie, what's takin' ya so long? Dad's got workin' on his mind."

"Coming. Carly, this is Cody."

"Hannah's brother?"

"Yes, I am. So you've already met my sister I see."

"Well, of course, she's a guest. She's gonna have two babies soon. She told me I could hold them after they're born. One day I'm gonna be a babysitter and make lots of money."

Maggie pressed her lips together to keep from laughing. Carly was a whirlwind, and there was no stranger to her. Before the day was over, she would have both Hannah and Cody's complete past. Then again maybe only Hannah's. Cody was very closed about his life, and Maggie couldn't help but wonder why.

Nathan came outside to greet Maggie and Cody. "You don't know how much I appreciate this. I'm so tired of repairing this house. I just want this over with."

"Yeah, we still have things to do in the barn." Carly scurried around her dad and into the living room where she said, "When we get through, Brady, I've got some new animals to show you. There's one dog that really needs a home."

Her son mumbled some reply, and knowing his present attitude, Maggie was glad she didn't hear it. "Point us in the right direction, and we'll get to work."

Later that afternoon with hot pink paint from Carly's room all over her, Maggie followed Nathan outside. Brady trudged behind them while Nathan's daughter skipped ahead of her dad. Cody remained in the house finishing the last touches to the dining room, while Hannah waited for her brother on the porch, taking a few minutes to rest.

Nathan opened the barn door and swept his arm in front of him. "As you can see, I'm trying to repair the pens and fenced area while at the same time expanding what we have and running my veterinary practice in Hope. There are so many animals that were left stranded after the hurricane and not enough places to put them."

"Daddy, you forgot there isn't enough people to adopt them."

Nathan tousled his daughter's red hair. "Yeah, you're right, pumpkin. Not from lack of work on your part, though."

Carly thrust out her chest. "I've got the most important job. I was doing good 'til school let out. A lot of the kids helped me." When Brady came into the barn, she tugged on his hand. "C'mon. I gotta show you this dog. We just got him. He reminds me of Frisky."

Brady threw Maggie a narrow-eyed look as his cousin dragged him out the back double doors. She decided she'd better follow. As she left the barn, she glimpsed Cody and Hannah coming in the other entrance. Cody looked about as bad as she did with muted green paint splotches on his old clothing as well as his arms and legs.

Carly gestured toward a large pen with a chain-link fence surrounding it. "There."

Brady peered at a black Lab. After a few seconds he looked away, his gaze latching on to another dog by itself hobbling across the pen toward him. Its ears perked, the mutt made its way to Brady on only two front legs. Her son entered the pen and squatted by the light brown dog. "Who is this?"

"That's Sadie. She's been with us for ages. Daddy found her after the hurricane and saved her life. You like her?"

Brady rose. "She gets around pretty good for only having two legs."

"I had to amputate the back ones or she would have died," Nathan said as he came out of the barn with Cody and Hannah.

Sadie sniffed Brady's hand dangling at his side and nudged it until he rubbed her behind the ears, but he kept his attention trained forward, not making eye contact with the animal.

"She's just now getting a handle on how to get about." Nathan held open the gate while the rest of them went into the pen with Carly and Brady.

"Do you see a dog you'd like to adopt?" Maggie scanned the rest of the animals—two goats and another curly white-haired dog no more than a foot tall—in the twelve-by-twelve pen.

"I don't want a pet." Brady took a step forward.

"We've got more out back in some other pens." Carly danced about, going from one animal to the next. "I can show you."

Sadie rubbed herself against Brady's leg, then nosed his hand. He glanced down, opened his mouth as though to say something but instead snapped it closed and knelt again at Sadie's side, petting her.

"Aren't you a cute one," Hannah said, stooping to pick up the fluffy white ball.

"Don't even think it, Hannah. Our apartment complex doesn't allow pets."

"Really? That's such a shame. She could use a home, too. You know, one of the first things I got when I was on my own was a cat."

Cody shot Maggie an exasperated look.

She chuckled. "I know that Mrs. Abare owns that small complex. I have a feeling, Cody, you could change her mind with some logical arguments in favor of the animal. She has a soft heart. Appeal to her sense of helping victims of the hurricane."

"A lot of times people don't realize animals are victims of disasters, too." Nathan settled his hand on Carly's shoulder. "I've been working on a way for Sadie to get around well. I'm almost finished making it."

"You should see it, Brady." Carly grabbed his hand again and began pulling him toward the gate.

Brady jerked away from the little girl. "Stop it." He tore past his cousin and slammed open the gate, then hurried toward the pasture.

Not sure what to do, Maggie just stared as her son planted himself at the fence at the end of the drive, leaning against the wooden slats. Words swam around in her mind, but she didn't know what to say to Brady. His body language screamed anger. At her for suggesting he get another pet? At what he had said in the car coming to the farm? Before she could move, Cody strode from the pen and headed toward her son.

She ran after Cody and caught up with him partway down the drive. "I appreciate what you want to do, but I have to be the one to talk to Brady. Once he gives Sadie a chance, he'll want her. I know my son. He loves animals. He used to help Nathan when he could, especially in the summer."

"I don't know if you should force Sadie on Brady."

"Spoken like a person who hasn't had a pet. They're therapeutic. You said so yourself."

"So you think Brady will be fine after he bonds with Sadie?"

"He'll focus on her problems, not his own. It works for me."

"Problems catch up with you if you don't deal with them." Intensity poured from Cody, his arms straight at his sides, his hands opening and closing.

"It sounds like you're talking from experience."

"Aren't most life lessons learned from our own mistakes?"

She peered toward her son, whose shoulders hunched forward, his head hanging down. "We'll have to debate this another time. I have a son to talk to."

"Don't just talk to him, listen, too."

"I know how to listen." Grinding her teeth together, she stalked toward her son. When she reached him, all words fled her mind. *Lord, I need Your help. What do I do? What do I say?*

"It's okay to be sad about Frisky. I miss him, too. He was a good pet."

"The best. No animal can replace him," Brady mumbled, his head bowed.

"You never really had time to grieve him. The hurricane struck and things got chaotic. I get that. Sadie doesn't have to replace Frisky in your heart. We have room to love many people, animals."

"Like God loves us?"

Where did that come from? "Is that what's wrong? You think the Lord has stopped loving us?"

He flailed his arms about. "Look what He did to Hope."

"And Hope is coming back better. We will be stronger."

"Until the next hurricane." Tears shone in her son's eyes.

Maggie stepped close and started to embrace him, to give him her love and comfort.

"Don't." Brady jerked away from her and stormed back toward Nathan's house.

He passed Cody who spoke to him, but Brady ignored him and kept going. Maggie sank back against the fence, thankful it was there to support her. Brady's anger still surrounded her in a viselike grip. She closed her eyes and took deep breaths that didn't really fill her lungs. The pressure about her chest squeezed even tighter.

"Maggie?"

She looked into the kindness in Cody's gaze and nearly went into his embrace. Grasping a slat of the fence to keep her still, she swallowed away the lump in her throat and said, "He's mad at God for the hurricane."

"I've heard that before. It doesn't surprise me.

It can be hard to understand why the Lord lets bad things happen to good people."

"Why does He?"

"Because this life is a time for us to learn and grow in our faith."

"And we learn through our pain?"

"Sometimes."

"All I know is that I hate seeing my son like he is, and I'm gonna do all I can to help him." She shoved herself away from the fence and marched back to Nathan standing with Hannah and Carly outside the animal pen. "I'd like to adopt Sadie."

Sunday afternoon Maggie spied Nathan's truck coming down the drive toward Bienville. She hurried from the upstairs gallery to wait for her cousin. Brady was holed up in his room, immediately going there after nibbling on his lunch until he managed to eat about a third of the sandwich. Sadie was the answer. She knew it in her heart. Cody didn't know her son as well as she did.

Nathan pulled around to the back of the house and hopped from the cab. "Since Carly went to a friend's after church, I finished the two-wheel cart for Sadie, so I could bring her over. I got another two animals yesterday after y'all left, so I'm glad you can take her early." He opened the back of his truck and jumped up into the bed to get the crate with Sadie.

When he handed it to Maggie, she placed it on the ground and let out their new pet. Sadie hung back in her crate. "C'mon, girl. This is your home now."

Nathan leaped to the ground, holding the two-wheel cart. "She doesn't like changes. It might take a while for her to come out. Just put the crate in a room and leave the door open. She'll exit eventually. Do you need my help getting her into the house?"

"I can do it. I know you have to pick up Carly. You two are welcome to come back for dinner. We're having our first dinner in the dining room this evening."

"It's a nice feeling having your house put back together."

"Yeah. You don't realize it until your place is a mess for months and months."

Nathan grinned and opened his door. "I appreciate your help and invitation, cuz, but I'm going home to eat in our dining room for the second time since Hurricane Naomi."

"See you later."

Maggie carried the crate and the small two-wheel cart through the back door into the newly renovated downstairs kitchen. Setting Sadie's carrier on the floor next to the contraption that Nathan made for the dog, she scanned the room. With all the rooms except one restored and Kim married to Zane and living with him, the house seemed almost empty. It would be good having a pet again. Maybe even another one after Sadie adjusted. She was so glad Uncle Keith loved animals, as well.

She knelt in front of the crate and tried to coax Sadie out. The dog hunkered down in the back with her tail wagging, but not budging. After getting a bowl of water and placing it right outside the carrier, Maggie washed her hands and started her Mexican chicken casserole for dinner.

Half an hour later while the chicken was boiling, she stirred the sauce on the stove, blending together the cream of chicken soup, onion, tomatoes and chilies.

"What's that doing here?"

She turned toward her son in the middle of the kitchen, staring at the crate with Sadie curled up in it. "I told you I wanted to give Sadie a home."

"But you didn't bring her home yesterday. I thought you meant later. And what's that?" He waved his hand at the two-wheel contraption.

"That's what Nathan made to help her get around better."

A whimper from the carrier pulled Brady to

it. He squatted down and looked inside. "You're okay, girl." Reaching in, he rubbed Sadie behind her ears. "C'mon out. You can't stay in there."

Sadie inched forward but still remained in the crate. While Maggie switched off the burner with the pot of sauce, Brady patted the floor right outside the carrier. Sadie crawled a little more toward him, stopping half a foot from the opening.

Brady rose. "Why won't she come out?"

"She's scared. This is all new for her. She's gone through a lot since the hurricane. She needs help."

Brady went to the refrigerator and grabbed an apple and a soft drink. "I know what you're doing. It won't work. Sadie's your pet. You wanted her so you can get her out." Then he started for the back door.

As he left, Sadie pulled herself out of the crate and toward where Brady was going. By the time she reached the door, Brady had left. Sadie looked up at the exit and barked.

Minutes passed, but Brady didn't return.

A pressure in her chest made Maggie doubt her decision to bring the dog home. Was Cody right? And yet, she remembered all the times her son had played with Frisky. He'd instantly bonded with the Lab when he'd seen him at the old vet's practice years ago, left abandoned on the doorstep of the office. "Sorry, Sadie. It may take some time for him to come around."

Whimpering, Sadie lay on the floor near the door, her gaze glued to it. Maggie stroked her hand down the length of the mutt's back. But the dog didn't even turn to look at her.

"Brady's just mad at me right now. He'll get over it in a day or so." *I hope.* There was a time when she would have been sure of that, when the bond between her and Brady had been strong. Now she didn't know.

After washing her hands, Maggie removed the corn tortillas from their package and turned on the burner to finish the sauce.

I don't know if you should force Sadie on Brady.

Cody's words taunted her. She wasn't forcing Brady really. Just giving him an opportunity to fall in love with Sadie.

But what if it wasn't the right move? What if Brady never came around? She glanced at the dog waiting for her son to return. At least she was out of the crate. Sadie turned her head toward Maggie as she moved the crate to the laundry room with the dish.

Her big brown eyes snagged Maggie's attention. She paused at the sadness she glimpsed in the dog's face. Sadie needed Brady as much as he needed her.

Chapter Six

Waving at Maggie from across the grassy lawn in front of City Hall, Hannah hurried toward her, with a smile on her face. Cody trailed behind his sister, stopping to talk to a couple people on the way. Maggie stepped out from behind the booth she manned at the Ultimate Garage Sale to give Hannah a hug. Cody's sister glowed with happiness.

"You look great." Maggie backed away to take a look at the young woman, wearing shorts and a T-shirt with sandals and a broad floppy hat to protect her fair skin. "Hope has been good for you."

"Zane hired me and I started work this past Wednesday. When I can't do electrical work anymore, I'll work in his office until after the babies are born. I'm working in Biloxi on a hotel. I know I owe it to you and Cody."

"Me?"

Hannah laughed. "Don't pretend you didn't say something to Zane. I know Cody did, too."

"Zane wouldn't hire someone for a construction job unless they're good at what they do."

"Getting a chance to meet him on the Fourth made me feel at ease when I went into the interview. That helped a lot. Thanks for at least inviting Cody and me to join you guys on the boat."

"That was Zane's doing." Maggie's gaze linked with Cody's as he approached them.

"What can I do to help?" Hannah took in the rows of tables with stacks of books and items donated for the library fundraiser. "People have really supported this."

"I've been amazed. So many lost their belongings, and yet they have found a way to help the town either with time or items. This has been advertised all along the coast. I'm in charge of the book section. I could use some extra help."

Cody came to a stop next to his sister. "You've got it. It'll give me time to peruse the books for any mystery ones. I want to pick out a good one for you to read."

Maggie snapped her finger. "That reminds me." She ducked behind the table and produced a thick romance book. "I loved this story. Let me know what you think after you finish it."

"Before the day's over you'll have your book to read." He scanned the rows of paperbacks. "I'm sure I can find something here."

"The mystery ones are over there." Maggie gestured toward the end of the table near her. "Have fun digging around in them. The money goes to a good cause. I've categorized a lot of the books by genres, but I haven't finished."

"I can help with that. Just point me to the pile you need me to look through," Hannah said.

Maggie waved her hand at three boxes she hadn't finished emptying. "If you could do those that would be great. I've got the sections labeled."

As Hannah moved to the cartons, Cody stepped closer. "Where's Brady?"

"Good question. He disappeared about an hour ago. Said something about looking around. The last time I saw him he was checking out the video games."

"How did it go with Sadie and Brady?"

"When he's downstairs, she follows him around. When he leaves the house, she lays by the door waiting for him to return. She's wearing him down. He's now petting her and actually spending some time playing with her, but most of his time is spent in his room. Sadie can't climb the stairs, so she doesn't see him much."

"Do you regret bringing her home?"

"No. She needed a family, and I think Brady will accept her eventually. I hope sooner than later. I don't like him spending so much time in his room, especially since I'm at work and Uncle Keith is gone more and more. In a couple weeks, Brady is supposed to help with Vacation Bible School at church, and he's complaining about that. He usually does a lot of activities, but he isn't this summer. I can't get him enthusiastic about anything. Not even fishing. That's a first."

"I'll find him and see what he's up to."

"I'd appreciate any help you can give me with him."

"Let me see what I can do." He started to leave but stopped and swung back to her. "I'm going to let you keep this book for me."

"Chicken. You don't want to carry the romance around?"

His eyes narrow on her, he turned the book over and over in his hands. "Is this a test?"

"I think of it more like a challenge."

"Then no problem."

The warmth of his expression wrapped about Maggie, and for a few seconds she forgot her problems with Brady and focused totally on Cody. When he left to search for her son, the romance clasped in his hand, she couldn't take her gaze off him until he disappeared into a busload of people from a large retirement community in Hattiesburg north of Hope.

Several of them headed for her tables. She greeted them and helped them find what they wanted. Thirty minutes and twenty customers later, she spied Cody threading his way through the throng toward her. A frown alerted her that something was wrong.

"Hannah, can you help this couple?"

Cody's sister nodded and took over while Maggie met Cody a few yards away.

"What's wrong?"

"I can't find Brady. I've looked all over, and no one has seen him. Keith saw him about fifteen minutes ago sitting on the bench under the live oak over there." He indicated a tree away from where the garage sale was.

"He knows not to leave the grounds of City Hall." But she remembered Brady's threat to walk home. She fumbled in her pocket for her cell and then punched in the phone number at the house. After the fifth ring, she left a message.

"He must be around here." Anxiety rumbled in her stomach, a nauseated feeling taking hold. She turned back to Hannah, lowering her voice so others didn't hear. "Cody and I are going to search for Brady. If he comes here, please have him wait for me."

"If I see him, I'll call Cody's cell."

"Great." Maggie joined Cody again and gestured to the left. "I'll go that way. You go to the right. Let's meet by the live oak."

As she scanned the area and stopped several people to see if they'd seen Brady, Maggie's heart began to beat faster and her breathing became labored as though she was stuck in a small space with no way out. Normally she wouldn't be concerned, but with her son lately she didn't know what to expect.

Cody paused at the table Kim manned for the garage sale. "Have you seen Brady?"

"No, but let me see if Anna has." Maggie's cousin waved toward her daughter talking with some of her friends a few yards away. When Anna came to the table, she asked, "Do you know where Brady went?"

"Yep. I saw him go inside City Hall."

"How long ago?" Cody glanced toward the double doors to the building.

Anna shrugged. "A while."

He handed the romance novel to Kim. "Here, keep this for me," he told her then he started for the building.

Kim laughed. "Maggie must have something to do with your selection of reading material."

He turned and backpedaled. "According to her, she's broadening my horizons."

When he went inside, he glimpsed Brady sitting on the stairs that swept down from the second floor. Cody halted and placed a call to Maggie. "He's inside City Hall."

"I'll be there," she said in a raspy voice.

"Give me some time to talk to him first. He's sitting on the stairs with his chin in his palm, looking like he's lost his best friend. Okay?"

Her deep sigh floated to him. "I'll wait. While I've been looking for him, one thing has become evident. He needs help whether he agrees or not."

"We'll talk about that later. Let me see what he says." Cody entered the main corridor, cool air enveloping him.

Brady stared at a step at the bottom. The sound of Cody's footsteps brought the boy's head up. His frown dissolved into a neutral expression like a mask falling into place.

"Hi. What are you doing in here?" Cody mounted the first stair.

"Hangin'."

Cody sat next to Brady. "It's cooler in here."

"Yeah. Mom won't let me go home."

"Are any of your friends here?"

"I guess. I saw a couple. They were going to the beach."

"You didn't want to?"

"Nope. Not interested."

Cody lounged back against the step behind him, propping himself up with his elbows. "You know what I would like to learn before I leave Hope? Floundering. Have you ever done that? Your mom says you like to fish."

With his forehead scrunched, Brady peered back at him for a few seconds. "Sure. Sometimes I have across the road from Bienville. That beach area is good for floundering at night."

"I've seen people doing that. So night is the best time to do it?"

"If you go gigging for flounder but you can fish for them using a rod, usually early in the morning."

"Have you gone gigging any this summer?"

Brady shook his head.

"Would you be interested in showing me how? I've enjoyed eating flounder and would love to learn how to catch it." Cody watched the play of emotions—from surprise to uncertainty—flitter across Brady's face, his expression finally settling back into a bland one.

"Why me?" Wariness edged his words.

Cody stared into the boy's eyes, clouding with his doubt. "Because your mother is worried about you."

"And she wants you to talk to me like you did with Uncle Keith?"

"Yes."

Brady shot to his feet. "I don't need no shrink. I'm fine." He started down the steps.

"Are you, Brady? Why are you spending so much time by yourself? Why are you avoiding your friends, even your family? Why have you given up doing what you've enjoyed doing in the past?"

Maggie's son whirled. "Because I want to. There's nothing wrong with spending time by yourself. Or doing something different from the same ole thing."

"No. It's good for people to spend time by themselves *some* of the time. But the reasons for doing it are what's important."

The sound of a door closing resonated through the silence. Brady glared at Cody as Maggie crossed the large foyer toward her son. When the child spun on his heel and stormed toward the door, Maggie tried to stop him.

He shook her off and said, "I'm okay. Leave me alone. I want to be alone. I'm not like Uncle Keith was."

The slamming door echoed through the air, as though Brady wanted to emphasize what he said with an exclamation mark. Maggie's shoulders sagged as she expelled a long breath. "That must not have gone well."

"He doesn't think he needs help."

"He's as stubborn as Uncle Keith. I'll have my uncle talk to him. Maybe he can persuade him to get help."

"He needs to want to see me. If he doesn't, it probably won't be effective."

"I'll let you know."

"Fine. Call if he agrees. I can still try anyway, if you want me to."

"Please do. I don't know what else to do. I feel my son slipping away from me. I know some moodiness is natural when kids become teen-agers, but every day it's becoming more evident *that* isn't what's going on here."

"I agree." He'd seen it in the boy's expression—something he'd glimpsed in others he'd counseled. A desperation. A sadness that pervaded his whole being. "I'll do what I can, and maybe Sadie will win him over," he said to offer some encouragement.

"He tries to stay away from her, but when he sees her, he can't. He doesn't want to care, but that's hard for him, so maybe in time she'll reach him."

"Animals have a way about them with people

who are hurting. They have an uncanny ability to sense that in a person."

"He's gonna be thirteen next Friday and he doesn't want to do anything for his birthday. He doesn't want to have a party, go out to dinner. Nothing. In the past his birthday has been a big deal."

That was the kind of thing that worried Cody. That and the fact that he didn't want to see his friends and spent most of his time in his room. He could remember as a young teen doing the same thing once. One too many moves had taken a toll on him, and he hadn't known how to deal with it. Until a youth minister at the church he went to had helped him.

He shoved to his feet. "C'mon. I still have a book to find for you."

"Where's yours?"

He looked down at his empty hands then up at her. "Kim has it."

"We'll go get it before someone I know forgets it." As Maggie exited the building, she scanned the people and relaxed some when she glimpsed her son with another kid. "Maybe something you said reached Brady. He's with Jesse. They're best friends."

Cody studied Maggie's son's body language. The boy was physically with Jesse, but mentally he seemed far away. He hoped Keith could get Brady to see him because denying he had a problem wouldn't help him.

On Tuesday afternoon, Brady prowled Cody's office as he had for the last fifteen minutes of their session, not saying more than a few words in answer to the questions Cody had asked him. The boy's body language—tense, glancing at the door, rubbing his thumbs and forefingers together—shouted he didn't want to be here.

Cody decided to change tactics. "The other day you said something about you taking me gigging for flounders. Are you still up for it?"

Brady turned from the large window that overlooked the front of City Hall and the Gulf in the distance. "You don't hafta do that. I'm not gonna talk about how I feel. Uncle Keith may have needed that, but I don't. I don't care what Uncle Keith and Mom think."

"No, that isn't the reason. I want to try it. As I told you, I love flounder. I've been interested in that way of fishing for them. Will you take me?" Cody prepared himself for Brady to say no, but the child cocked his head and thought for a moment.

"Yeah, why not. It'll keep Mom happy and it's certainly better than sitting in here."

"That's great. Then I can get your mom to show me how to cook them."

"I'll only take you on one condition. No talking about feelings," the child said, pursing his lips as though he had swallowed something distasteful. "Mom is overprotective and worries too much."

"I have found mothers do that with their children. Kinda comes with the territory."

"How about Friday night?"

"Isn't that your birthday?"

"I don't want any fuss about that. What's the big deal about turning thirteen? Now when I turn eighteen, it'll be different."

"Doesn't your mom have something planned for Friday night?"

"Yeah, dinner. We can go after that. It needs to be dark anyway."

Cody rose. "I look forward to it."

"Come to dinner and then we can leave right after that."

Was that so Brady wouldn't have to interact with his family? "So long as it's okay with your mom." Cody would check with Maggie about dinner and going out gigging for flounders on Friday night. He didn't want to interfere with family plans. For a few seconds he thought back to his childhood and his family. It had been years since he'd had any sense of a family. With Hannah back living with him, he'd begun to remember what he'd been missing. But it seemed God had plans for him that didn't involve a family.

"Is there anything else?" Rocking back and forth, Brady glanced at the wall clock, impatience stamped on his features.

"No, but I'm here if you ever do need to talk."

The slanted look he gave Cody as Brady marched toward the exit, head down, made it evident that wouldn't happen anytime soon. Out in the hall the boy hurried toward his mother's office at the end of the corridor.

Through the open doorway, Cody caught Maggie's expectant gaze. He shook his head slowly. The corners of her mouth inched downward until her son went through the entrance and Cody could see Maggie struggle to smile, the usual sparkle in her eyes gone.

He went back into his office, blowing out an exasperated breath. He'd wanted to be able to unlock the child's pain and get him to talk. But he also knew he couldn't help Brady until he saw a need for that help. Right now the child felt he was alone and forging by himself through his anxiety, most likely produced from grief over all the changes in his life lately.

The disappointment on Maggie's face haunted

Cody as he prepared for his next appointment. He couldn't get her out of his mind and that bothered him.

Friday evening, Maggie tossed another sundress onto her bed, still not settled on the perfect outfit to wear for Brady's birthday dinner. She wanted everything to be special for her son.

Who am I kidding? Yes, I want that, but all I've been thinking about is Cody coming tonight.

On her bedside table, she caught sight of the book Cody had given her to read, C.S. Lewis's *The Lion, the Witch and the Wardrobe.* At first she'd thought it was more a child's story, but soon it captured her interest. She was almost finished. Where was Cody in her book? She wouldn't be surprised if he hadn't even started it.

At City Hall earlier, he'd walked down the stairs with her as she'd left work instead of using the elevator. He'd even escorted her to her Dodge Charger. Mostly they had talked about Hannah and how she was enjoying her job. But as he'd reached around to open her car door, he'd paused and locked gazes with her, so close she could smell a hint of his lime-scented aftershave and the peppermint candies he enjoyed throughout the day. She'd thought of asking him about the romance novel then, but bound to his look, she couldn't think of anything coherent to say. He'd left before she'd realized she'd lost her chance.

Even now she imagined the aromas of lime and peppermint teasing her senses. She grasped her last sundress—a white one with colorful flowers—and slipped it over her head, her fingers quivering slightly as she buttoned it up the front. Positioned before her full-length mirror on the back of the closet door, she assessed herself. The dress flared out from her waist, falling just above her knees. A bright yellow belt clinched her waist. The colors accentuated her tan from working outside in the garden.

Suddenly she pivoted away from the mirror. She never worried about what she wore. Why now? She didn't like the answer that came to her mind. Cody. But he was only passing through Hope.

Remember that. Get emotionally involved and he'll hurt you.

She slid into her white sandals and left her bedroom, determined to keep Cody Weston at arm's length. She still thought he could help Brady. If only her son would agree. At least after dinner, Brady was taking Cody gigging for flounders. Maybe it would work after all.

Nearing the kitchen downstairs, she heard Uncle Keith's raised voice and stopped, not wanting to disturb him. Then Brady cut in with, "That was you. It's not me. Why is everyone on my case?"

Before she could move from the doorway, her son charged out of the room and stomped past her with Sadie hurrying to keep up with him. His glare told Maggie all she needed to know. Uncle Keith had said something else to him about getting help.

She entered the room, zeroing in on her uncle sitting at the table. His thick eyebrows scrunched together in a frown.

"Your son has the Sommerfield stubbornness."

Maggie pressed her lips together to keep from smiling. Her uncle was certainly known for his. "You're his role model."

"Poor child. I tried to get him to understand it was okay to ask for help. He didn't need to learn that the hard way like me. I'm worried about him."

"So am I. But what else can I do?"

Uncle Keith shook his head. "I wish I knew the answer to that. Making him won't work. It didn't with me."

Yelping from the front of the house drew Maggie's attention. "He left Sadie downstairs again. She so wants to go upstairs after Brady."

She started toward the staircase when Sadie's

barking stopped. Moving down the hallway, Maggie heard Brady talking to the dog. She slowed and peeked around the corner. Brady held Sadie in his lap while he sat at the bottom of the steps, stroking her and murmuring something to the dog that she couldn't hear clearly. Relieved he'd paid attention this time, she backed away.

The sound of the chimes echoed through the house. Through the glass panels on the sides of the double doors, she saw Hannah, which meant Cody was here. As she crossed the foyer, her pulse kicked up its tempo while Brady picked up Sadie and carried her toward the back area.

"Hi, glad y'all could come tonight." Maggie's glance skimmed down Cody's length.

Dressed in tan shorts, a navy blue polo shirt and brown sandals, he looked relaxed. And handsome and charming.

Don't go there, Maggie.

Pushing thoughts of the man from her mind, she focused on Hannah. "You must be busy. I haven't seen you since last weekend. Is Zane overworking you?"

Hannah smiled. "Not at all. I've enjoyed using my skills again and I plan to continue for as long as I can."

"If she has anything to say, it'll be right up to the end," Cody said. The concern Maggie heard in his voice struck a chord in her. She and her brother didn't have that kind of relationship. Her extended family was loving but not her immediate one. All through her childhood there had been a wall between her mother and her, often putting her father in the middle. She could remember the strain in the house when her dad had taken her side on things.

"When squatting, crawling through attics and climbing ladders gets too much, I'll gladly work in Zane's office. I won't do anything to endanger my babies. I'm still having a hard time realizing I'll have twins." Hannah splayed her hand over her chest. "Just the thought sends my heart racing."

"It would mine. Being a parent isn't easy." Maggie closed the door behind them as they came into the house.

Hannah's eyes widened.

Maggie quickly added, "But you'll be able to do it. We'll help." But the second she said it, she peered at Cody and wondered when he would have to leave and go to another disaster site. Hannah had mentioned staying here possibly. How did Cody feel? Did he want his sister to stay in Hope or go with him?

"I see Brady is spending time with Sadie."

Cody gestured toward the back of the house where her son had disappeared with the dog.

"Sort of. This is the first time he's come back down to play with Sadie when she barks at the bottom of the stairs."

"That's progress. Sadie's amazing. She's getting around well."

"But she can't do stairs. It frustrates her. She tried yesterday, and I finally had to pick her up and take her to my bedroom. She ran out of it and sat in front of Brady's door. He finally let her in for a while."

"Sounds like she's slowly wearing him down," Cody said as he followed her and Hannah down the hallway.

"If he was himself, that wouldn't be an issue," Maggie whispered so Brady wouldn't overhear. Louder she added, "Uncle Keith is in the kitchen. The rest of the guests should be arriving soon."

"Where's Ruth?" Cody asked when he entered the room.

"She's watching her grandsons for Kathleen and Gideon. They're all coming together." Uncle Keith stood. "Wanna help me, Cody? We're gonna grill hamburgers out back. Zane brought over his grill earlier so we'll have two going."

"Sure."

As the two men left the kitchen, the front door-bell rang again.

"Be right back." Maggie strode toward the foyer. In the past her son's birthday had always been a time for celebration, but this year Brady wasn't cooperating. It seemed the last place he wanted to be was in the middle of a party in his honor. This was the time she missed Robbie the most—when she needed someone to lean on and discuss Brady and his problems.

When she tried to imagine Robbie, all she could picture was Cody, telling her that he would help her. She shook his image from her mind and opened the front door.

Cody changed into some cutoff jeans and a T-shirt to go gigging with Brady. He stuffed his other clothes in a backpack and went in search of Maggie. He wasn't leaving without talking to her, no matter how much she'd tried to avoid him during the dinner. Finding her in the kitchen, he paused and watched her for a moment until she spied him and stopped rinsing off the dishes.

"I'm glad you changed. Floundering can get messy." Maggie turned back to the counter.

"You're okay with Brady and me going gig-ging across the road?"

She placed more plates into the sink. "Sure.

As I told you, as long as he stayed until after the cake and presents, it's fine."

"Come with us." The invitation was out of his mouth before he thought about it. He missed talking with her this evening. She'd been playing the hostess while trying to coax her son into participating in his own birthday party.

"I have guests to see to. I'd better not. Besides, my son didn't invite me." She faced him, her expression not revealing anything.

Cody bridged the distance between them. "Brady didn't exactly invite me, either. I invited myself. I think he's doing it to prove he's all right."

Deep furrows grooved the space between her eyebrows. "You think he's all right then?"

"No, he's struggling, but he doesn't want anyone to know it."

"It's kinda hard not to see it. He isn't the same boy he was before the hurricane."

"I know it. You know it. But he doesn't. At least he hasn't admitted it to himself yet."

"I told Hannah if she didn't want to wait around until you returned that I'd take her home."

"Yeah, she told me." For the past few hours Maggie had talked with Hannah a lot. But this was the most she'd spoken to him. That bothered him, and he wished it didn't.

"I'm almost finished with the book you gave me. I've enjoyed it." She paused then asked, "Have you read the romance yet?"

"I knew I forgot something. I finished it last night."

"And?"

"Interesting, especially how people's pasts influence their decisions."

"You got that from the book? I felt it was about forgiveness."

"That, too." He looked toward the back door. "I'd better go on outside and meet up with Brady or he might leave me behind."

"I'm glad he's fishing. Well, in this case going gigging. He hasn't done that in a long time even though his friends have asked."

"Did he say anything about our session on Tuesday?"

"Yes, but nothing that surprised me. He told me he wasn't going back. I would have been surprised if he hadn't said that. It was the first thing out of his mouth when he came into my office afterward."

No wonder he'd glimpsed worry and sadness in her eyes when he had seen her. "I wish I could have done more, but he isn't ready to talk."

"What if he's never ready?"

Loved ones had asked that question many

times over the years when he dealt with troubled people. "That's a possibility but often something triggers a need for help."

"Like with Uncle Keith."

"Yes. All we can do is be here for him and pray Brady sees he needs help."

"We?"

"I'll be here to help."

"What happens when you leave?"

"We'll deal with that when it happens." A cop-out, he realized, but he didn't know what else to say.

"Sure. Why worry until you have to." Her tone held a forced lightness to it that didn't reach the shadows in her eyes.

Shadows that drew him toward her until only inches separated them. "I wish I had all the answers. I don't. It's very frustrating. Wanting to help and not being able to." He attempted a smile that didn't stay long on his mouth.

"I've wished that. Probably every parent has." She dropped her head, her hair falling forward to hide her expression. When she looked up again, uncertainty remained in her gaze.

He hooked the errant strands of hair behind her ear then cradled her face in his hands. "You have a lot of people in the other room who care about you and Brady. Even if I leave, there are others who can help your son. But I'm not going anywhere for a few months." Why did saying that *not* make him happy? Because he cared about her and Brady. Because… He wasn't going there. He'd been through this once with Beth and made the decision not to go through it again.

He let his arms fall to his sides while stepping away. "I'd better go see where Brady is."

She swung around and headed for the exit into the hallway. "Yes, you'd better do that."

Her rigid back, like a well-constructed wall, proclaimed her displeasure. He'd had no business touching her like that. His action conveyed something he wasn't prepared to admit. He committed himself to his clients. That was about all he could do since he'd avoided anything more all his life. Commitment led to complications—an emotional mess that he found best to avoid if he wanted to help others.

"I enjoyed tonight. I haven't been to a birthday celebration in ages," Hannah said as Maggie pulled into the parking space in front of Cody's apartment. "I appreciate the ride home. I have to be at work early tomorrow."

"You're working long hours?"

"As many as the supervisor will give me. I

need to save up for the babies so, as long as I feel all right to work, I'm going to."

"I can understand that. What does Cody say about that?"

"He's like a mother hen. Concerned I'm overdoing it. I keep telling him pregnant women aren't fragile."

"Cody believes that?"

"Not usually, but what I do and what other women do is different to my brother."

Maybe it was because Cody was older whereas her brother was younger, but she'd never felt protected and watched over by Eli. Regretting what she couldn't change, she chewed her bottom lip, wondering where her only brother was now. Even though she didn't see her father, she knew where he was. Then again, what good did that do? They didn't have a relationship. Her immediate family was a real mess. "It's nice that you have Cody."

"But look at you. Everyone there tonight cared about each other. Your uncle, cousins. Cody and I lost touch with our extended family. They are strangers to us."

"What are you going to do when Cody has to leave for his next assignment? Have you and Cody talked about it?"

Hannah clasped her hands and twisted them in her lap, the glow from the security light in the parking lot illuminating her agitation. "I don't know and that's a problem. Cody and I have avoided that subject. I'm not sure either one of us knows what would be best."

"If you need to talk to someone, I'm here for you."

"Thanks. I might take you up on that. Cody isn't the best one to go to for advice that concerns him." Hannah shoved open the door and slid out of the car. Leaning down, she smiled. "I like Hope, and I haven't even been here that long. What's gonna happen when I'm here for months?"

"Maybe you'll find a home." Could Cody do that? Did he even know how to?

"I'd like to. I can't see taking two newborns to some of the places Cody goes." She shut the car door and leaned in the open window. "Don't keep my big brother out too late. He has to drive me to work tomorrow morning. That's the first thing I'm gonna get—a used car. I sold mine months ago to use the money to live on, but when Cody leaves, I'll need transportation no matter where I am." She smiled. "Good night."

As Hannah left, Maggie watched her until she went into the apartment. *When* he leaves. Not *if* he leaves. That thought caused her heart to ache. She backed out of the parking space and drove toward Bienville. Driving down the highway that ran along the beach, she wallowed deep in thought till she glimpsed a light out in the water. Cody and Brady searching for flounders.

Suddenly she wrenched the steering wheel to the right and pulled into the parking area between the road and beach. Her son and Cody were out in the shallow water about a hundred feet from shore. After taking off her sandals, she ran across the warm sand, the heat of the day still retained in it. She dropped her shoes a few yards from the breaking waves and splashed into the sea, heading toward the light Brady held.

Cody speared something in the water. "I got one."

"It's about time." Her son actually laughed. "We'd starve if you were in charge of gathering food."

"Good thing I never signed up for any reality shows."

"You'd be voted off."

The back-and-forth between Cody and Brady made her pause. She almost hated disturbing them, but then Brady saw her and waved.

"Mom, come join us."

"Glad you took me up on coming, although I don't know if I would have worn a sundress." Cody's gaze traveled down her length, leaving a warmth that had nothing to do with the ninety-degree temperature.

She stopped a few feet from them. "A spur-of-the-moment decision. The water isn't even up to the top of my calves. I'm fine." She peeked into the floating foam chest. "Only one flounder and it's kinda small."

"I'm just getting into the groove." Cody scanned the seabed around him.

"Yeah, Mom, he's a slow learner. He almost gigged his foot."

"Ouch. That would hurt," Maggie said with a chuckle.

"I was in control. I knew what I was doing. These flounder are tricky. I think they see the light and know someone is trying to get them and hightail it out of here." Cody gestured toward the area illuminated by the lamp. "See, no flounders."

"Then we keep moving. We're bound to run into some. Slow and steady works best. Someone here splashed their way from shore, alerting every fish around to get out of the way." Her son pointedly looked at her, but a twinkle of merriment glittered in his eyes.

The look on her son's face, full of teasing, gave her hope that he was responding to Cody. "Okay. You got me. I haven't done this since I was a child. I forgot the protocol. But I'm a fast learner. It won't be a problem in the future." She swept her gaze to Cody. "Contrary to some."

"I accept the challenge. Brady, why don't you give your mother the other gig and let's see who gets the biggest flounder. Okay?"

She nodded. "If I win, what do I get?"

"What do you think?"

"A favor to be determined."

"You want me to accept without knowing what it will be?"

"I promise it won't go against your beliefs."

"Okay, and if I win, I get a favor to be determined."

Suddenly she realized the mistake in her challenge. Bantering with Cody was easy, but the consequences might be too much. "So long as it doesn't go against my beliefs."

"Done. Let's go."

Maggie took the gig from Brady and started out. "Oh, I forgot to tell you I used to be quite good at this."

Cody howled with laughter.

She glanced over her shoulder at him. "You need to be quiet. You're scaring the fish away."

"Mom, by now the flounders are buried deep in the sand. That's one of their defenses, Cody."

She turned around and walked backward while

she said, "That's okay. There's usually a faint outline you can see when you know what to look for. Brady might help you with that."

Her next step back sent her scrambling for footing.

Chapter Seven

One second Maggie stood in below-the-knee water and the next submerged in it when the sea floor dropped off.

Laughter, from both Brady and Cody, echoed through the night. She got her footing, now up to her chest in the Gulf. Gig in one hand, she swiped her other across her face to flip her wet hair out of her eyes. Then she looked at her son and Cody, who were trying to contain their merriment and not doing a good job.

"Just a temporary setback. I forgot about that drop-off." Holding down her sundress, Maggie waded to the shallower area.

"We can call it a night if you want." Cody compressed his lips together into a tight line while her son continued laughing.

She loved hearing that sound from Brady, but enough was enough. "I guess—"

"Of course, I'll be the winner by default."

"I was gonna say a little dunking isn't gonna stop me. Game on."

One hour later, Brady called it. "You both have three flounders, the biggest ones about the same size so it's a tie."

"I think we should weigh them," Maggie said as she headed toward shore.

Cody leaned close to her and whispered, "At least Brady participated."

"I notice he waited until you caught that last big fish to call the contest. My son the peacemaker."

"We could settle on a tie."

"My flounder weighs more." She slanted a look at him, so close she swallowed hard. "I didn't get wet for nothing. I already have my favor planned." Adopting a dog from Nathan would be good for him. Then she thought of how well Sadie was working out and wondered if she should make Cody adopting an animal her favor.

An eyebrow went up. "You do? What?"

"I'm not telling you until after we weigh the flounder and I win officially. Then you'll know." She gave him a smile and a wink.

Holding the lantern while Brady carried the container with the fish, Cody chuckled. "I didn't know you were so competitive. An interesting side to you."

"You aren't?"

"I didn't say that. I know I'm going to win and I only wanted to give you an out."

"Hey, you two," Brady called out. "Let's go. I've gotta take care of these fish."

"He's going to do that?" Cody trudged across the beach toward where Brady was waiting for them.

"Uncle Keith taught him if you fish you have to clean them. I'm glad to see he remembers that because I hate to clean them."

"And I'm glad he's doing what he's supposed to."

"Maybe he's getting better. This past hour or so I actually saw my old son again."

Cody slowed his step. "But the problem is still there, Maggie. He'll need to deal with it."

"That's what I was afraid you'd say."

"Sorry. I've seen the ups and downs in people too many times."

At her car Maggie opened her trunk for Cody and Brady to stow the gear and cooler before they climbed inside her Dodge. Minutes later, she pulled up at the back of the house, and Brady hopped out as soon as she popped the trunk.

Maggie exited the car and mounted the steps.

"I'll get the scales. Don't put the fish together yet, Brady. I don't want my prize-winning catch to get mixed up with Cody's smaller ones."

She found the scales in the storeroom off the kitchen and hurried back out, turning on the light for Brady to clean the fish later. He'd already grabbed his knife and the wooden cutting board he had used in the past.

Her son took her biggest flounder and weighed it, having each of them check his figure. "Don't want any complaints from the loser." Then he placed Cody's on the scale. "It looks like this one weighs almost an ounce more."

"Almost?" Maggie leaned in and double checked the number. "Okay, I lost. What's the favor you want me to do?" Ignoring Cody's smirk, she moved away from the overpowering fish smell as Brady started cleaning the flounders.

"I'd like you to prepare mine for me. I've never cooked a flounder, and I know Hannah hasn't either."

"What if I haven't?"

"I figure you have since Brady has gone gigging in the past and you're a good cook. I'm not. My food is edible, most of the time. That's all I can say."

"Thankfully I have and I have a good recipe I use. How about you and Hannah come over on

Sunday evening, and I'll prepare all of them for everyone? We usually have a big family meal then."

"Are you sure we aren't intruding?"

"We can pretend I won instead."

"Nope."

"You and Hannah aren't intruding. I wouldn't have suggested it if you were. But if you have something else in mind, fine."

"How about you come tomorrow to my apartment and cook mine?"

"Your place? Why?"

"Because you need a break. You planned a big birthday celebration tonight. You don't need another big dinner two days later."

Cooking for him at his apartment, even with Hannah there, sounded so much more intimate. As she reminded herself to keep up her defenses, the word no was on the tip of her tongue but what came out was, "What time do you want to eat tomorrow?"

"How about seven?"

"Fine. I'll be there at five-thirty to get it ready."

He shortened the distance between them, which made a mockery of her earlier declaration. "What was the favor you wanted from me if you won?"

"I may be easy to read, especially for a counselor, but a gal has got to have some mystery about her."

"In other words, you aren't telling me."

"You are sharp. Now I'd better get inside and change out of this wet dress. Good night."

When she escaped into the kitchen, she knelt to greet Sadie, rubbing her behind the ears. "I shouldn't have challenged him. What am I gonna do? The more I'm around Cody, the more I like him."

Sadie barked her reply.

"Yeah, that's what I was thinking. Not a wise thing."

Cody sat across from Maggie at the table in his small dining room. What had he been thinking when he had invited her to cook for him this evening? At the time he'd thought his sister would be here, and he would be safe from wishing there was more between Maggie and him. In the past he'd wished that too many times to be foolish enough to do so again. There came a time when he'd numbed himself from caring too much.

He looked at Maggie but her head was down as she finished her last few bites and he couldn't see her expression. But he didn't need to. He knew the soft glow of the overhead light cast a golden hue over her features, beckoning him to forget what had happened in the past.

She'd spent an hour preparing her baked flounder au gratin, the cheese complementing the fish perfectly. He'd never had a seafood dish that tasted any better. Why wasn't she married? From all he'd seen, she would be a great partner for any man. What held her back?

Deflecting that dangerous line of thinking, he introduced a tamer subject. "Too bad Hannah missed this. She loves seafood."

Maggie peered up, her long dark lashes veiling her eyes. "I thought she was going to be here."

"So did I. Turns out some of the people at work go out a couple times a month for dinner and they invited her to go, too."

"It'll be good for her to get to know others. When you leave—"

"She'll come with me. I know that's the best now. She'll need help with the babies. One is hard enough by yourself, but she's having twins."

Maggie stabbed him with her sharp look. "Believe me, I'm aware of the challenges. Have you talked to her about when you have to leave?"

"When she first came, but we haven't talked about it since. I don't want her to get too settled. It'll be harder for her to leave."

"Is that what you do each time you go to a new place?"

"Yes." Today he'd gotten notification he was third on the roster to go to the next disaster. With hurricane season picking up that could be a month away if there was a bad year like a few years ago. That only reconfirmed why he did what he did with each relocation.

Maggie rose and began stacking the dishes. "I saved some fish for Hannah to try tomorrow. There's enough for you, too." Moving toward the kitchen, she didn't make eye contact. In fact, she seemed to be purposely looking away from him. Was there something she wasn't telling him?

He stood and gathered the glasses and silverware then followed her. "Have you and Hannah talked about what she's going to do when I have to leave?"

"I think she's considering staying here."

"Why? She hasn't lived here long. What's here for her?"

"What's out there for her?" Maggie countered.

"Me. I'm her family. I can help her with the twins. The more I'm getting used to the situation, the more I feel that way."

"There's a reason she didn't want to go with you when she graduated from high school in Los Angeles. You need to talk to her again. I told her I would help if she decided to stay. Hope is a good town. She has a job she enjoys. She has—"

"How can you really help her when she needs it? You have your own life. She'll need support. She'll need…" Words fled his mind as Maggie's eyes narrowed, her hands tightened on the dishes she held.

"Having my own life doesn't mean I can't help. We're becoming friends."

He thumped his chest. "I'm her brother." His voice rose several decibels.

Maggie stepped back and shook her head. "Why are we arguing?"

Because I think Hannah will stay in Hope, and now I realize I don't want to leave her behind. Having her around made him realize how much he'd missed her the past few years. He'd gotten used to being alone, but Hannah's presence made him realize how lonely he'd been.

"After all," Maggie continued, "it's Hannah's decision in the long run."

"How can she make that kind of decision when she'll be here only a couple months?"

"What's really behind this, Cody? You're asking her to pick up and go place to place with you. How's that any different?"

"Look, this discussion wasn't my intent for

this evening." The tension in his neck burned a path down his spine.

"What was your intent?"

"To have a home-cooked meal."

She finally put the dishes she held into the sink. "You would have had that if you came tomorrow night for dinner."

"I wanted to spend some time with you. When we usually see each other, there are a lot of other people around." There, he'd admitted what he hadn't been able to say for the past few weeks. He was attracted to her. Surely he could get to know her and keep their relationship on a friendly basis only. He should be able to prevent those feelings from developing any deeper. He certainly had enough experience doing that.

Her huge eyes transfixed him. He cut the distance between them by half. *Run before it's too late. Leave.* Then the thought that he couldn't leave because this was his apartment caused a chuckle to rumble in his chest. He was tired of keeping himself apart from people.

His gaze glued to her full lips, he inched forward as if invisible ropes pulled him closer. Her mouth enticed him. He couldn't resist. The space between them gone, he held her face and kissed her, a soft brush of his lips against hers that evolved into an assault of the senses. Her scent flooded him. The feel of her skin against his palms heightened his awareness of her. The rhythmic rise and fall of her breathing matched his increasingly fast tempo.

In the distance he heard a noise—something he should acknowledge—but he couldn't. All he wanted to do was continue the kiss.

Until the sound of a throat clearing sent Maggie flying back, her cheeks flushed with a deep red. She stared behind him. He spun around.

Poised in the doorway to the kitchen, Hannah took a step away. "Sorry. I didn't mean to interrupt anything."

Maggie grabbed her purse from the counter. "You didn't. I was just leaving."

He reached out to stop her, and his hand caught air. "Great timing," he murmured as he passed his sister and went after Maggie.

"I thought so," Hannah called after him.

Halfway to Maggie's car, he caught up with her. "Don't leave."

She slowed her pace, whirling around and pedaling backward. "I have to be at church early tomorrow. The favor didn't say anything about the dishes, so I figured you could handle it."

"Sure." He shouldn't have kissed her.

"Talk with your sister about her plans," Maggie

said, putting a damper on the past few minutes. She turned around and practically ran to her car.

Cody stood still, watching her. By avoiding involvement with people over the years, somehow he'd lost his ability to relate to a woman on a level other than as counselor to a client. He definitely didn't want that with Maggie.

When she pulled away in her Dodge, he trudged back into the apartment, preparing to face another woman in his life. He hoped he was more successful. He needed to make Hannah understand she would need his support. They were family, and she didn't have to go through giving birth to twins alone.

Inside his apartment he found Hannah in the kitchen. "How was your evening?"

"I enjoyed dinner together with people from work. Zane's secretary is funny and will be nice to work with when I have to report to the office. Getting to know her makes me feel better about that."

"I haven't had a chance to tell you that I heard from headquarters. I'm third in the rotation. We might have to leave as soon as a month or so." His breath caught in his throat as he waited for her to respond.

"So soon?"

"That's the nature of my job."

"How do you do it?"

"I remember all the people I help who need it." Cody leaned against the doorjamb, his arms crossed over his chest.

"You can help people anywhere you want. There will always be others who need counseling. You're gifted in that, but you don't have to travel around to do it."

"The people I help are facing desperate times. Often they have lost everything."

"That can happen anywhere without a disaster occurring."

"What are you getting at?"

Hannah opened the refrigerator and removed a carton of milk. "I might not come with you. In L.A. I got a taste of what it's like to be in a place for over three years. I like making friends and knowing I'll be around six months later. I like being me and not holding myself back. I've seen you. That's what you do."

"You can't stay here. You'll need help with the twins. You need family. Having two babies is a big responsibility."

"Believe me, I'm finding that out." She poured a tall glass of milk. "I'm not fond of milk, but I drink at least two glasses a day." When she took a swallow, a grimace pursed her face.

"I want to be part of your children's lives."

"And I want that, too. But I have to decide what's best for me and my kids. I don't want to put them through what you and I went through. Look what it has done to you. You won't let others see the real Cody. You keep yourself locked away."

"It sounds like you've already decided." Gritting his teeth, he straightened from the doorjamb.

"I'm leaning toward staying in Hope. I like it here. Maggie is becoming a friend. I have a nice job with an employer who appreciates a female electrician. I've not always had that in the time I've been working in the field."

"I want you to feel you can depend on family. We moved around a lot, but we had each other while growing up. Our parents usually were there for us."

Hannah placed her glass on the counter, closed the space between them and hugged Cody. "I know I can depend on you if I need it. I'm learning to stand on my own two feet, but remember my children and I will always have room for you in our lives. I want them to know you and love you. So stop in Hope between assignments if you can."

"Sure," he murmured, not really sure if he could keep returning to Hope for a brief visit then moving on again. "I'll keep you informed as I move up the rotation list. Please let me know when you make up your mind."

"I will. Who knows? I'm so emotional right now I could change my mind by morning. I could decide to go back to California and look up the father of these babies and demand he do something. Not that it will help."

"You need to let him know where you are and that you're having twins."

"I know. I just haven't figured out how or when. There's a part of me that doesn't think I owe him any explanation. He walked out on me and *my* babies." She patted her rounded stomach. "That's how I feel. These babies are mine, not ours or his." She walked back to pick up her milk. "I'm gonna finish this and go to bed. It's been a long day, and I told Maggie I would go to church tomorrow. She's gonna teach me how to knit and wants to introduce me to her group of ladies who make prayer shawls. She says when she knits she forgets her worries and concentrates on the stitches. I might need something like that in the future."

"Great. I'm glad you're going to church."

"I want to see what the attraction is for you and Maggie."

As Hannah left him in the kitchen, Maggie's name rang through his mind. He'd kissed her this evening. He shouldn't have. It had sent a message to her that he cared. Although he did, she deserved more than that. When his mother had died in a disaster, he'd made a promise to God he would make a difference in the lives of people who suffered. Maggie deserved someone who would be around.

Sitting in the game room too keyed up to go to bed, Maggie worked on a shawl. She only had a little left to do. She'd finish it and take it to church with her tomorrow. She knew a woman who needed it and would be there.

But after taking out another row of stitches, she wasn't so sure knitting was a good idea. She couldn't stop thinking about Cody kissing her tonight. Shaking from the memory, she put her needles and shawl in her lap and clasped her hands together to still the trembling.

She'd wanted the kiss to go on and on. The second their lips had touched she'd experienced a sense of coming home. But that wasn't really the case. Cody didn't even know what it meant to have a home. He had wanderlust in his blood.

But still, the kiss…

She laid her head on the back cushion of the couch and stared at the ceiling.

"I thought you would be in bed by now."

With a gasp, Maggie shot up straight.

Ruth came into the room. "I was heading downstairs when I saw the light on in here. I thought it might be Brady."

"No, he went to bed hours ago. Get this, with Sadie staying in his room for the first time. She was one happy dog when he carried her upstairs."

"Oh, good." Ruth took the chair across from Maggie. "I'm glad he's warming to Sadie. She needs him, and he needs her."

"I think so, too, but I was beginning to have doubts about my plan."

"Sometimes you can't plan those kind of things."

"Tell me about it. He may still change his mind. Brady hasn't been doing what he normally does. It's hard to tell what he's going to do."

"When I came in, you looked like you had lost your best friend. What's going on?"

"My son not doing well isn't enough for me to be worried?"

"You had dinner with Cody tonight. How did it go?"

Hands still clasped, Maggie tightened her hold until her knuckles whitened.

"Aah, I've hit a sore spot. You like Cody Weston."

"Of course I do. He helped Uncle Keith, and he's now trying to help Brady even though my son doesn't want any help. Doesn't think anything is wrong."

"Sounds like another stubborn man in this family."

"Yeah, Brady certainly learned the wrong thing from Uncle Keith."

"Over the past months working closely with you at City Hall, I've learned to read you. As much as I know you're concerned about Brady, I think that frown has to do with something—or someone—else."

"Cody kissed me tonight."

Both of Ruth's eyebrows hiked up. "And you didn't want him to?"

"Let's say I was surprised—pleasantly." That was putting it mildly. She still blushed when she thought about the kiss and that had been hours ago.

"So what's the problem? He's not married. You aren't either. Maybe something will come of it. Take it from this newly wedded lady, being married is wonderful." A glow spread over Ruth's face.

Maggie eased the grip her hands had on each other and shook one loose. "I'm glad you believe that since I think Uncle Keith is extra special."

"More than that. He gives me a reason to wake up each morning. For the longest time I'd forgotten what it meant to be married. Cody would be a wonderful father for Brady."

Maggie's mouth dropped open. "It was just a kiss. He didn't propose marriage, and he isn't likely to. He told me tonight he's slated to leave Hope soon."

Ruth straightened in her chair. "When? That's the first I heard." She fluttered her hand in the air. "Oh, I know he was sent to us by the Christian Assistance Coalition, but I was getting used to seeing him at City Hall every day. I thought maybe he would stay. We don't have anyone like him in Hope. He fills a need."

"People will be sad to see him leave." Definitely she would be. When she thought about it, sadness enveloped her, making it nearly impossible to work as the still unfinished shawl in her lap attested.

"It sounds like you feel that way, so say something to him about staying. We could use a counselor of his caliber."

"No, I would never ask someone to stay who doesn't want to." It hadn't worked with Robbie. She'd tried to get him not to re-up in the army, but he had wanted the training they were providing.

Ruth leaned forward, her elbows on her thighs, her eyes fastened on to Maggie's face. "What are you not telling me? When you care about a person, you need to let them know that."

"Cody's a friend. That's all."

"I think he's more. When you mentioned the kiss, a look came into your eyes that said he could be more than a friend."

Maggie shoved to her feet, the shawl and needles falling to the floor. "I won't ever ask a man to stay again."

"Again? When did you do that?"

"Robbie. I didn't want him to sign up again for the army. He did anyway and look what happened. I was left alone to raise Brady. My son will never know his father. He didn't care how I felt."

"It sounds like you're still angry with Robbie."

Tears unexpectedly welled up into her eyes. "If he hadn't gone, he would still be alive today, and we would be married. I wasn't important enough to him." Feelings she'd held inside rose to the surface. She'd never shared that insight with anyone because she hadn't realized the depth of her anger at Robbie for leaving and then dying.

She blinked to rid her eyes of her tears but more flowed, rolling down her cheeks. "Excuse me." After snatching up the shawl and needles on the floor, she hurried away.

"Maggie."

She halted in the doorway and glanced back.

"Robbie didn't purposefully abandon you. He wasn't your parents. And Cody isn't Robbie or your parents."

"From where I stand the end result is the same. They left. I'm alone." Maggie fled into the hallway. What had she been holding inside for all these years?

Cody looked up the stairs between the second and third floor of City Hall to see Maggie descend. In the past three days since he'd kissed her, she had avoided him, and he hadn't gone to see her because he wasn't sure what to say or do. He'd made sure not to place himself in a situation like Saturday night, confused and questioning himself.

Her gaze riveted to him. Her expression neutral, she nodded as she passed him on the steps.

He couldn't let it go. "Maggie, how are you?"

She stopped and swiveled toward him. "Fine. You?"

"Fine." *If that includes thinking about you way more than I should. Picturing your flushed face after the kiss at the oddest times during the day.*

"Good. I've got to go. The city council's meeting is starting, and I have to be there from the beginning to take notes." She held up the laptop she carried.

"Maybe we can grab lunch this week." Why did he ask her that? He still didn't know what to say to her or what he should do next. In the past, it had been so much easier to walk away. Why was this so different? Probably he'd been working too hard and needed a break. He hadn't had a vacation in eighteen months.

"That would be nice," she finally said then continued her trek down the stairs to the second floor where the city council met once a month, her steps light and quick.

He walked up to the third floor, strode to his office, pulled out a stale sandwich from yesterday to eat for lunch and flipped open a file of a man he was concerned about. He'd lost his home and business in the hurricane and was still going through the angry stage of grief for those losses. There were many people in Hope struggling. The economy hadn't been great even before the hurricane hit. Now it was barely limping along since the primary moneymaking industry, tourism, was suffering.

Fifteen minutes later with his sandwich finished and his notes on the client's case jotted down on a pad, Cody closed the file and put it on a stack. He had a few more to go through before his next appointment.

A noise from the entrance of his small office attracted his attention to the open door, left that way when he wasn't with a client so people knew he was available. Brady stood just inside the room, his eyes red, his face pale.

Cody bolted to his feet and skirted his desk. "What's wrong?"

Chapter Eight

"Sadie is gone. I've looked for her and can't find her." Brady opened and closed his hands at his sides. "It's my fault she's missing. I wasn't paying attention."

"Come in." Cody waved at a chair not far from the boy. "Tell me what happened. How'd you get here?"

"Ran." Brady remained still, sweat glistening his face, his shirt damp from it.

But what drew Cody to the boy was the lower lip quivering, the sheen in his eyes. Brady was barely holding himself together.

"I need help finding Sadie. Mom isn't in her office. Where is she? I tried calling her cell. She isn't answering." Panic laced each word. Brady's hands now fisted so tightly his knuckles were white.

"She's in a city council meeting." Schooling

his voice into a calm cadence, Cody half sat, half leaned against the front of his desk.

The teen pivoted. "On the second floor?"

"Yes, but I'll help you. We can find Sadie."

"I need to get back to the house and look."

Cody plucked his car keys from his desktop and headed out into the hall. "I'll drive."

"But what about Mom?"

"By the time her meeting is over, hopefully we'll have Sadie back."

Ten minutes later, Cody pulled into the Bienville driveway. "Where's Keith?"

Brady wrung his hands over and over. "I don't know. Maybe his men's group at church. I shouldn't have gone to the Quick and Go. I left her on the back porch. She has never gone down the stairs without me carrying her. I looked all around the second-floor gallery. She isn't anywhere up there. I don't know how she made it down the stairs." The boy chattered almost nonstop, his words coming out in a steady stream.

Cody parked behind the antebellum house. "She went down those stairs?" He pointed to the steep ones from the second story.

"Yeah, that's the only way she could have used. She could have hurt herself. I told her I was gonna be right back." Brady shoved open the door and leaped from the vehicle. "I know she can get around the house, but out here? What if she tried to cross a street? She can't run to get out of the way of a car coming."

The frantic ring to the boy's words prompted Cody to reassure him. He said in a soothing voice, "We'll find her. Maybe she tried to follow you."

He shook his head. "I didn't see her coming back. What if someone took her?"

"I'll call your uncle Keith. He can help us. Did you leave a message on your mom's cell?"

"No."

"Okay. I'll leave one and let her know what's happening."

While Cody dug into his pocket for his cell, Brady murmured, "I should have taken her with me. She's always trying to follow me. She's probably lost and doesn't know how to get back here. She hasn't been here long. Or, what if she is hurt somewhere? She's been through so much. Nathan said she should have died after the hurricane. But she didn't. Now she might because of me."

"Brady." He waited until he had the boy's attention before continuing. "You did all you could. You left her where you thought she would be safe. She hasn't been gone long so that means she's probably nearby."

"I hope so." Brady scrubbed his hands down his face.

After Cody placed the two calls, he walked to Brady who paced from the hood of Cody's car to the trunk. "C'mon. Let's check the yard. Your uncle is coming home with some of his friends. They'll be here in a few minutes."

Brady peered up at Cody with tears in his eyes. "I could have gotten the cart. Maybe tied a rope to it like a leash. If something happens to her..." His voice faded on a quivering thread. The boy gulped and hunched his shoulders, his head down.

"Listen, Brady. A lot of people are going to help you. Sadie probably hasn't gone far. She's smart. If she can't find you, she'll come home."

The hard line of Brady's mouth proclaimed he didn't believe what Cody was saying. He stomped toward the neighbor's place to the left. "They have a pit bull that sometimes gets out. Let's check there first."

When Maggie returned to her office to begin cleaning up the minutes she took at the city council meeting, she checked her cell that she'd put on silent. She had a missed call from Brady but no message and one from Cody. With a message. She tried Brady at the house but no one answered. It obviously wasn't important enough for him to leave a message, so she laid her cell on the desktop and settled behind her computer to work.

She wasn't ready to return Cody's call, probably to firm a lunch date for this week. She didn't know if she should go. What use was it? He would leave; she would stay. Their outlooks on life were too different. Hers revolved around her family and friends; his around his work. The past few days she'd lost enough sleep because of him. Right now she had work to do. She'd wait until this evening to call Cody back.

But after only a few minutes, she paused and looked at the phone. Maybe she should listen to Cody's message. He didn't usually call her. If he had something to say, he'd come by her office. When she'd glanced toward his office, the door was closed. He was either gone or in a therapy session.

If that was the case, she didn't want to disturb him. No, she'd wait and see if the door opened.

But her mind kept pulling her back to her cell. Finally she played the message.

"Maggie, Brady came to City Hall today upset. Sadie has gone off. I'm out helping him look for the dog."

She checked her watch. Four o'clock. As she

rose to talk with the mayor, the door to her inner office opened.

Ruth clicked off her cell. "Keith called me to tell me they're looking for Sadie. Did you know she was lost?"

"I just found out. I was going to see if I could leave an hour early. I can make up the time later this week."

"Make up the time? You put in enough over-time to have the whole day off. I'm going with you. Brady was starting to bond with Sadie. I don't want to see anything happen to her."

Maggie grabbed her purse. "Thanks. I'll see you at the house."

When she arrived at Bienville, no one was around. She placed a call to Cody who answered immediately.

"We fanned out in all directions from the house. Brady is with me. We checked to make sure Sadie didn't get tangled up with the pit bull next door. He's been inside all day. We'll find her. We're letting the neighborhood know she's lost."

"Where are you?"

"At Sixth and Pelican Cove, near the Quick and Go."

"I'm coming."

"You might walk down Sunset Road. We were going to come back that way."

"Meet you there."

She hung up and hurried inside to change her heels to tennis shoes. When she came back outside, Ruth was getting out of her car. "I'm heading for Sunset Road," Maggie said. "I'm meeting Cody and Brady there."

"Great. I'll come with you. Keith called again and said his group of men from church haven't had any success. No one has seen Sadie. They've been talking to neighbors, anyone they see."

As they walked toward Sunset Road, Ruth asked, "Have you given any more thought to what we talked about Saturday night?"

Maggie wanted to laugh. That was about all she had thought about for the past few days, which was why she hadn't been sleeping well. "Yes, but it hasn't done any good. How do you change years of responding and thinking one thing? I know Robbie did what he thought was right, but that doesn't change my feelings. I felt abandoned just like when my parents left Hope. They cut me out of their lives. I made a mistake and that was all they could focus on. My mom didn't surprise me, but my dad did."

"Robbie wouldn't have made that choice if he'd known it would have taken him away from you. He left not knowing you were pregnant. His decision may have been different if he'd known that. Starting a family makes a man think differently. All I can say is take it one step at a time. We can't change overnight—at least not easily. I'm always telling Keith I'm a work in progress when we argue about something."

"You're newlyweds."

Ruth chuckled. "Newlyweds argue. Believe me. Especially two strong-willed people like Keith and me. We haven't been married for many years and we'd forgotten what an adjustment it can be. We're two old fogies set in our ways."

Maggie scanned Sunset Road. No evidence of Sadie anywhere. She'd known once Brady allowed himself to care about Sadie he would one hundred percent. She'd thought that would be a good thing for her son. But she should have remembered what it was like to love someone and have that someone leave you, even if it wasn't willingly. It hurt—a hurt that touched your very being. Her stomach clenched at the prospects of telling her son his pet was nowhere to be found.

"Did Uncle Keith find her?" Brady asked as he made his way to the intersection of Sixth and Sunset Road.

Cody returned his cell phone to his pocket. "No, he was letting me know where he and his friends have searched."

"And they've found nothin'?" With a scowl deepening the grooves in his face, Maggie's son surged forward on the sidewalk. He went a few yards then swung around and screamed, "Why is this happening? What have I done wrong to deserve all of this? We could have lost our home. Any more water or wind and we would have. Gone." He snapped his fingers. "Just like that."

Cody moved forward. "Hope lost a lot this last year," he said in an even tone.

"Look at Sadie. She lost her two back legs and now she's gone. She can't protect herself. She needs me." Brady's voice rose even more. "My best friend lost his house. Another friend lost a cousin. Swept away by the water. I don't understand...." He opened his mouth to say something else, but no words came out. His face turned beet-red.

Cody planted himself in front of the boy, and started to reach toward him.

All of a sudden Brady flew at him, his fists pounding into Cody's chest. "Why? Why?" Sobs accompanied each word, wrenched from Brady.

Cody enclosed him in his arms and said repeatedly, "Let it out. You can tell me anything."

A shudder passed through the boy into Cody. The gut-ripping sobs coming from Brady gradually abated until he stood perfectly still, his arms finally dropping to his sides, as though his energy had fizzled out.

Cody spied Maggie running around the corner. He shook his head slightly and held up a palm. "Anything, Brady."

The boy stepped back, his eyes red and swollen. "I hate God. He did this to us."

Cody had heard that before. It never surprised him. People often lashed out at the Lord as if He had caused all their problems. Cody kept his expression neutral, his voice level. "Let me help you. We can talk about that and what's going on. Life is full of changes—some good, some bad. I want to teach you to deal with them. I guarantee the one thing that won't change is that life never stays the same."

"Why can't it?"

"That's a good question. As you grow up, would you want to stay in the same situation you're in? You'll want to leave your home and go out into the world."

Brady lowered his head and stared at the sidewalk.

Cody glanced at Maggie and Ruth at the end of the block, waiting. Worry marked Maggie's features with deep lines as she chewed her lower lip.

"Let's continue our search for Sadie. We'll talk about this later. Okay?"

After a long moment, Brady nodded.

Cody signaled with his hand for Maggie and Ruth to approach. "Good. Your mom and your aunt Ruth are here to help us."

Brady wiped his eyes then slowly rotated toward the women.

Maggie rushed the last few steps. "Are you okay?"

"No, I want Sadie. I didn't treat her the way I should. I need another chance, Mom."

Maggie slung her arm around her son and began walking toward Sunset Road. "Then let's keep looking."

"Did you see anything down Sunset Road?" Cody asked, falling into step with Ruth beside him.

"No, but we might search in the woods behind Bienville that leads down to the river."

Brady peered up at Maggie. "But there's a fence at the back of our property."

"She could have gone around in one of the neighbors' yards that isn't fenced."

"Yeah, she might have." Brady increased his pace, charging out ahead of Maggie.

She looked back at Cody and said, "Good thing I wore my tennis shoes," then jogged forward to keep up with her son.

A laugh escaped Ruth. "I should have changed

my shoes. These heels aren't high. Gave that up a long time ago, but I can't jog in them. If you want to go with them, I'll take up the rear."

"I'll hang back with you," Cody said.

"Good. We can pray we find Sadie."

Maggie watched Brady run ahead toward the fence along the property line in back. Downed trees and large branches still littered the ground from the hurricane. It was hard to maneuver through with the dead vegetation everywhere, but Sadie might have. *Please let us find her, Lord. Brady doesn't hate You. He's mad and hurting.*

"Mom, there's a hole in the fence back here. She could have wiggled through it."

Maggie caught up with her son at the chain-link barrier. "I forgot that needs mending. We've been working so hard on the house it slipped all of our minds."

Brady started climbing over the fence. Wearing a skirt, Maggie took a look and wondered how far she'd have to walk to find a break in the fence. When her son hopped to the ground and took off, she made a snap decision. "Wait up," she shouted.

After carefully scaling the chain link, using the holes for her feet, she perched on top and leaped to the ground, tumbling into a mud puddle nearby. "You realize the land is probably swampy the nearer we get to the river."

Brady's eyes grew round. "What about an alligator? There have been a few sighted back here over the years."

He would have to remind her of that fact. A tingle of apprehension streaked through her. "Let's wait for Cody."

"Aah, Mom, I'd take care of any critters that bother you."

"I know you would, but I'd still like to wait for him. A few more minutes won't matter."

"It could to Sadie."

"Here comes Ruth and him now. No more waiting."

Brady rocked back and forth, barely containing his energy as the pair crossed the yard. Cody made a running start and vaulted over the three-foot fence.

"I'm impressed," Maggie said when he landed on his feet, inches from another puddle.

"I'll stay here and let Keith and the others know what you're doing." Ruth fluttered her hand, urging them to search.

Brady dove into the vegetation.

"Stay in sight, Brady," Maggie said as she picked her way more carefully through the debris of dead branches and new foliage growing since the hurricane.

As Cody fanned out from here, Maggie called his name. "Sadie knows her name. Maybe we should shout it."

Maggie delved into the forest, taking turns calling Sadie along with Cody and Brady, then pausing to listen afterward. Yards ahead of her and Cody, Brady came to a stop and glanced back at them with his finger up to his lips. Then he shouted again.

In the distance Maggie heard a faint yelp. She hurried her steps as Brady began to race in the direction of the sound, continuing to yell to Sadie.

The underbrush scratched Maggie's legs as she increased her speed. Cody came from an angle and kept pace with her.

"Mom! Cody! Over here. She's stuck in a mud hole."

When Maggie broke through the vegetation and found Brady trying to dig his dog out of the mud, her heart swelled into her throat.

Cody rushed forward to help her son. Sadie tried to move, but her lower part sunk below the surface of gooey, thick brown mud. Brady tried to still her frantic movements and got licked in return. While Cody worked on her back end stuck in the mud, Brady leaned down and rubbed his chin along her face oblivious to the dirt smearing him. "I'm here. You're okay now."

When Sadie was finally freed, she scrambled into Brady's arms as fast as her two legs would carry her. He stood with her mud-crusted body plastered to his white T-shirt, a goofy grin on his face.

"What were you thinking, girl?" he asked with a chuckle in his voice as though he didn't care one way or another now that she was safe. "I've gotta give you a bath. I hope you like water."

Maggie strolled next to Cody, who was dirty halfway to his elbows. "People pay big money for a mud bath."

"I don't see the draw, but I would have gotten in knee-deep to get her out if I had to."

"Thank you for your help today," she said. "When things settle down, I want you to tell me what happened. I heard him screaming at you and came running."

"He's angry at God. He feels He abandoned him."

"I imagine others feel that way, too."

"Yes. They don't want to hear that the Lord is right there with them through the rough times. They want everything fixed immediately. It's hard going through those times, but we usually come out of them tougher and better able to deal with life in general. I try to help people see ways to learn from the experiences and to deal with their feelings."

"Dealing with feelings can be tough, especially if we don't always realize why we feel a certain way." She recalled her conversation with Ruth about Robbie abandoning her like her parents. Emotions she'd suppressed even from herself had come to the surface. Now she had to figure out how to handle them. "Will he let you help him?"

"People have to reach a certain place before they are ready for counseling. I think he realized that today. Sadie's disappearance illustrated all he'd been going through and trying to ignore since the hurricane. I don't think he can ignore it anymore."

"Then hopefully the healing can begin." Now that she realized she had been harboring angry feelings toward Robbie for signing up for the army again which led to his death, could she begin to heal, too? She'd been hanging on to them for almost fourteen years. Remembering the sorrow and pain cautioned her. Knowing she should change didn't mean she would.

She peered at his attire then hers. "We look a sight, covered in mud and in my case scratches. I've learned no hiking through woods in a dress."

"Or gigging for flounders. Life is a continuous learning experience."

"Sometimes I have to be knocked over the head to get what I need." Ruth's words came back to her. *When you care about a person, you need to let them know that.* She cared about Cody—too much. She wasn't ready to let him know that. He'd spent his life avoiding long-term relationships—for good reason—but they were exactly what she needed. Exactly what she hadn't gotten from her parents or Robbie. She wouldn't settle for less than that.

When they got to the house Brady placed Sadie on the ground near the hose, then turned on the outside faucet to begin cleaning her.

Maggie faced Cody. "I'm going to get cleaned up, too."

"We all need to talk. I'll go home, clean up, then come back. Okay?"

"You can stay for dinner if you want. Tonight I'm ordering in pizza. No cooking for me."

"You order pizza?"

She grinned. "From time to time, mostly because Brady loves pizza."

"Most kids do."

"Tell you a secret." She leaned close and whispered, "I do, too."

"See you in a little bit." Cody strode to his car.

"Mom, will you watch Sadie for a second? I've got to get a towel to dry her off."

Maggie stooped down to the wet dog. "If I didn't know better, I would have thought you planned this whole thing," she crooned to Sadie as she scratched behind her ear. "You see it, too. He's hurting. He needs you."

Sadie barked and rubbed her dripping body up against Maggie's muddy legs. She laughed. "Brady isn't gonna be too happy to see you're dirty right after your bath. But somehow I don't think he's gonna mind washing you again."

Maggie shut the dishwasher and switched it on. The back door opened, and Sadie came trotting in with Brady and Cody right behind her.

"Did you get the fence fixed?" she asked as she folded the washcloth over the faucet.

"She won't get to the woods through our yard. We took some wire and wove it through the chain links to hold it together." Brady removed the cart from Sadie then scooped her into his arms. "I'm taking her upstairs. She may be able to get down the steps but not up them."

When her son left the kitchen, she looked toward Cody and mouthed the words, "How did it go?"

"Good." He paused until he heard the sound of

footsteps on the staircase. "He's agreed to meet with me."

"Great. When do I bring him to your office?"

"We aren't meeting in my office. I've asked him to take me fishing around Hope. I figure he knows some good spots."

"Yes, but—"

"If he's doing something he's loved to do in the past, he'll feel more at ease with me." He quirked a grin. "Besides, I enjoyed floundering so I think I'd like to learn to fish."

"You've never fished?"

"As a child I was never real crazy about eating fish."

"But you ate the flounder."

"That's different. My tastes have changed."

"When's your first fishing trip?" She opened the refrigerator and took out a pitcher of iced tea. "Want some?"

"No, I need to head home soon." While she poured herself a glass, he continued. "This Saturday. He says we should go early in the morning, so I'm picking him up at six."

"Six! My son hasn't gotten up before nine or ten any day this summer. I'll get up and fix y'all some breakfast."

"You don't have to do that."

"I know. I want to. It's the least I can do if

you can help Brady. What you two talk about is confidential, but if there's something I need to know, I hope you'll tell me." Maggie wanted to sit in on the sessions between Cody and Brady, but she knew that wouldn't be a good idea. The older her son became, the less he shared with her even though she'd reassured him that nothing would ever come between them. She would never turn him away like her parents had done to her.

"With Brady's permission, I will. He has to feel what we discuss stays between us unless he says otherwise."

"That's fair."

"I'd better go." He started for the door, then turned back to Maggie. "You know initially I wasn't sure about Sadie being good for Brady, but I was wrong. Once he decided to care, he dove right in. She seems to be able to read his moods well. She was right there beside him as we fixed the fence."

"I'm glad because when his pet died right before the hurricane it was hard on him, then the storm hit and it just got worse. I don't know if he ever grieved Frisky's death."

"After seeing how Brady responds to animals, I realize that had to be hard on him. A lot was thrown at him in a short time."

"I probably didn't help the situation. I threw

myself into cleaning up the house and trying to put everything back to the way it was. I thought that would take care of everything." As she recalled those sixteen-hour workdays, she shook her head. "With Uncle Keith falling apart, I tried to do what I could to help him. Brady did, too. I don't regret doing that, but I also should have been more attuned to my son's needs."

Cody closed the space between them. "How about you? Did you ever stop to take care of yourself? Deal with your own feelings concerning the upheaval?"

"I'm fine," she murmured but immediately wondered if that was really true. Was she?

He stared at her as though probing into her mind to see what she was actually feeling. The true answer to his questions. "Are you?"

"Okay, if you must know, I will be when my son is better. He's my only concern."

"I understand that, but in order to take care of another, you must also take care of yourself."

Stiffening, she stepped back. "I don't need your services, counselor."

"I'm not offering my counseling services, but I am offering to be a friend who will listen when you need to vent. I think you've been so focused on helping everyone else that you're ignoring your needs."

"I don't have any."

"Everyone does."

Anger bubbled in her stomach. So now she was supposed to add her problems to the pile on top of everyone else's? "I could say the same thing to you. How can you do what you do day in and day out without being affected by it? You don't even have someone to share it with. You move from place to place, listening to other people's problems, trying to help them deal the best way they can. Who listens to yours? Who helps you?"

"I don't have—"

She held up her hand. "Don't tell me you don't have problems. If you think that, you're fooling yourself. Everyone has problems. That's life."

"My focus right now is Brady." Tension vibrated off him, his lips pressing together.

Anytime she had tried to delve into his life, he had slammed the door in her face. A person didn't do that unless there was a problem—something he wanted to forget. But it still held a grip on him. Maybe he wasn't even aware it did. Maggie inhaled a calming breath, realizing no good would come out of pushing him. He had shutting down to an art form. "I agree my son is my focus, too. If there is anything I can do, I will."

Cody glanced away for a long moment.

Silence hung between them, fraught with emotions Maggie suspected neither one wanted to acknowledge. The only sound that invaded the quiet was the ticking of the clock on the wall.

With a sigh, he turned his attention back to her. "Brady told me one of his cousins died in the hurricane," he said in his counselor voice, all business.

"Yes, Nathan's wife. We've talked about it, but Brady never said much about Caroline."

"That will give me something to start with him on Saturday." Cody walked toward the back door.

Maggie followed him to lock up after he left. "What do I do? I need to do something."

He pivoted toward her, his professional facade in place. "What you're doing now. Being there for him. Letting him know you love him. Life is pretty insecure for him right now. He needs to know he can count on you."

And the Lord. She could still remember hearing her son declare earlier that he hated God.

Cody moved through the doorway onto the veranda that wrapped around the house. Behind him the sun had sunk below the trees, a dimness creeping across the landscape as night approached.

She clutched the door. "Thanks. I feel like I'm saying that to you a lot lately."

"Me, too. Hannah and I had a talk about when I have to leave Hope."

"Is she staying?"

"She hasn't made up her mind."

"Have you ever thought about staying in a place like Hope? We could use a good counselor. There are people here who need help. It's not like there won't be another threat of a hurricane in the future, and I don't see the economy getting any better anytime soon."

"Open my own practice? No, I hadn't thought about that." Cody couldn't lie. He hadn't thought about that until recently. "Somehow I'll make sure Hannah has what she needs if I leave and she stays. I think though she will realize she needs family around her when she has her twins. And I'm it as far as family goes." He tapped his chest. In that moment he realized how much he was wanting Hannah to go with him. The more he thought about her two babies, the more he knew that he needed to be in their lives. To have a family again.

"You need to be prepared if she won't go with you. If she'll stay here."

"I've been doing that all my life."

"Preparing yourself to leave people behind?"

He nodded.

"How sad."

The pity he glimpsed in her eyes sent anger racing through him. He wanted to shout "I don't have to have people and a place to be happy," but the words wouldn't dislodge from his tight throat. Finally he stepped back, out of the light pouring from the kitchen. "We'll agree to disagree. I have a good life. I get to help people who need me." He'd promised God after his mother had died that he would, if He would just take the hurt away. God had—at least He had dulled it— and they had moved from the town not a month later. He hadn't been confronted with memories from his surroundings and had managed to let his pain go. He still was managing that painful time in his childhood.

"But are you ever really involved in these people's lives?"

He couldn't take any more of her questions tonight, her not-so-subtle probings. "Good night, Maggie." He backed up until he was at the stairs, feeling her gaze drill into him. Then he pivoted and strode to his car.

When she shut the door, his chest constricted and he finally released a bottled breath. Filling his lungs with fresh air, he climbed into his vehicle. Conflicting feelings twisted his gut. Why did Maggie always challenge him to be more involved with others? Wasn't he involved enough?

He certainly knew a lot of details of people's lives—some closely guarded. Plowing his hands through his hair, he looked toward the house. But was that really the same?

Especially when he had his own closely guarded secret he'd only shared with the Lord.

Chapter Nine

Two Saturdays later, Cody finished hammering in the last piece of vinyl siding and took a swig from his water bottle, then mopped his forehead and neck with a towel. "Now that I'm through, I'm finally getting the hang of hitting the nail instead of my thumb."

Zane stepped back from the addition they'd built to hold classrooms at a church in a neighboring town. "I'm glad you could fill in for Gideon at the last minute. I didn't want to postpone this mini-mission trip to Victory Christian Church. The kids needed it."

"I needed this." Cody joined Zane and surveyed the work the youth group had accomplished in the past four hours. After nine months the addition now stood where the old set of classrooms had been destroyed by Hurricane Naomi. The congregation had barely repaired their place of worship and had no funds for the rest of the construction. "I've been involved in a lot of disasters, but I'm usually wrapped up in helping the people pull themselves together—not the physical structures."

"They can often go hand in hand."

Cody scanned the smiling and laughing congregation assisting the Hope Community Church's teenagers. "I agree." In his head he'd known that, but seeing it in practice reinforced its impact.

"I didn't know if Brady would participate much, but he seems to be getting into it. I've heard about your couple fishing trips with him."

"From him?" Cody asked.

"No, from Kim who learned about them from Maggie."

"Speaking of Maggie and Kim, when are they bringing lunch for all of us?"

"At any moment."

"Good. I haven't done this much physical work in a long time. I need fuel."

The sound of tires crunching the gravel road that led to the church in the midst of a pine forest sliced the air.

Cody spied his sister in the car with Kim and Maggie. "Hannah didn't mention she was coming out here."

"Yeah, she asked me about it when I visited

the hotel project in Biloxi. I told her she was welcome to come. That I was sure there would be some wiring to be done."

When Hannah had first come to Hope, she'd told Cody everything that was going on in her life. Now he rarely saw her. She'd become involved in the shawl ministry at the church while learning to knit from Maggie. She'd gone out with some of her coworkers. About the only time he got to see her was when they happened to be working on the same project, especially now that she had bought a used car and didn't even need him to drive her to work.

"Maybe I should check with you to see what my sister is up to."

Zane cocked his head and stared at him. "That almost sounds like jealousy."

"She's not living with me, then all of a sudden she is. Now I never see her, and I'm beginning to wonder if she's sharing the apartment or not."

"She fits in great with the crew and their wives. I think the women have taken her under their wing since she's expecting. And my secretary can't wait until she comes to the main office to work with her. When you leave, you won't have to worry about Hannah. She'll be taken care of."

"Yeah, that's what Maggie tells me." As he

said her name, he searched her out in the group of teens mobbing the trio with the food.

Her hair pulled back in a ponytail, she handed a cooler to Brady then reached into the trunk for a box that she gave to another youth group member. Her son said something to her, and she laughed. The faint sound drifted on the light breeze and zinged him. He loved hearing her laughter and soft Southern drawl. She could be tough as nails then as sweet as the tea she served. Anyone who could teach Hannah to knit was gifted in his book. Just last night he'd seen the shawl his sister was working on. It wasn't bad, which surprised him. Hannah usually wasn't patient. But then he hadn't been around her much for over three years. Maybe she'd changed more than he thought. What else had he missed in his only immediate family member's life?

Maggie cupped her hands and shouted, "Hey, come help us."

For a second he didn't realize she was referring to him until Zane nudged him. "We're being summoned, and I've learned in my short married life not to ignore it."

"It looks like you've taken to it." Cody strode with Zane toward the Dodge loaded with food for the volunteers.

"Yep and I haven't regretted one second of

giving up my bachelorhood. You should give it a try some day."

"Maybe one day when I'm your age."

"Ouch. I'm only three years older than you."

The same age as Maggie. She should be married. What was holding her back? They had talked about a lot of things but never that. And why did he want her married? When he began thinking about another man with her, his gut knotted. He couldn't have it both ways. He wasn't what she needed. She wanted to know everything about a person. He didn't know how to do that because he'd stopped doing that a long time ago.

When Cody reached the Dodge, Maggie passed him a box of food. "Y'all have done a great job. We're staying this afternoon to help, too."

"I seem to recall you're good at painting."

"Myself? Or the wall?"

"Both."

A bark sounded.

Cody peered into the backseat. "You brought Sadie?"

"Yeah. She was wondering where Brady was. The past couple of weeks y'all have taken her with you fishing. She's used to being with Brady and doesn't understand when he's gone for long hours."

"And you know this how?"

"You should see her. She sits by the door he leaves through and won't move until he comes home. Well, at least, that's what she did this morning."

"So you concluded she was missing him?"

"That's what happens when you care about someone and you don't see them. You pine for them."

More than you know. Until you force yourself not to get involved, to suppress those feelings. He clamped his teeth together and took the box to the picnic area under the large live oak with long, thick branches that encompassed a wide expanse. When he'd first come to Hope in November, he'd seen so many trees stripped of their leaves, not because of winter but the storm. It was nice to see them recover—like the town. Which meant his time in Hope was coming to an end.

Maggie lifted Sadie out of the backseat, followed by her cart. After being strapped into it, Sadie took off after Brady, yelping the whole way. Her son spied his pet and scooped her up into his arms, cart and all.

Cody came up behind her and leaned close. "Once he gave himself permission to love another dog, he hasn't turned back."

"I'm so glad he did. I see glimpses of my son before the hurricane."

"I'm hopeful he'll get there."

"So the fishing sessions have been successful?"

"Yeah and you've seen the fish we've caught. That was hugely successful. I could get into fishing."

She faced him. "Do you have a hobby besides reading?"

"I run. It helps clear my mind."

"Is that all?" the woman, who had more hobbies than three people, asked.

"It fills my life. That and work."

"Yeah, if you say so."

He started to ask her about that comment, but Brady, with Sadie right behind him, headed toward them. "I'm starved."

"Help yourself." Maggie trailed after her son and gathered the youth group together to say a prayer.

The second she said amen, the kids rushed the food and drinks. Five minutes later everyone had what they wanted and were seated around the grounds, mingling with the congregation.

Cody grabbed a sandwich and found a place to sit under a magnolia tree dripping with huge white blossoms. The flowers scented the surroundings with their sweetness.

When Maggie joined him, he asked the question he started to right before Brady came over for his lunch. "What's wrong with reading and running as a hobby?"

"Nothing, but they're such solitary activities." She tilted her head, her forehead wrinkling. "Unless you're running with others. Do you? Do you enter races?"

"No. You read. Don't tell me you read your books out loud to others."

Maggie took a bite of her sandwich. When she finished chewing, she finally answered, "As a matter of fact, I do sometimes read to the ladies at the nursing home. They love a good romance. They can hardly wait until I come back to read the next chapter."

"Why do you feel like you have to surround yourself with people?"

Her eyes widened. "I don't have—" Clamping her mouth shut, she nibbled on her bottom lip. "Okay, I guess I usually do things with others. I like people. I love listening to their stories, getting to know them."

"Sorta like a therapist."

"I guess so. But don't worry. I'd never threaten your job."

He chuckled. "I wasn't worried. I'll be able to leave Hope in your capable hands."

"Oh, no. I wouldn't even begin to claim to

do what you do." She paused for a few seconds. "But answer me this. Why do you have to remind yourself and others you're leaving?"

Her question surprised him. He'd never thought about what he was doing. But she was right. It was something he did when he went to a new place—remind himself he was leaving in so many months. "A defensive tactic."

"So you see it, too."

"See what?"

"That you're an observer more than a participant in life."

He opened his mouth to refute her statement, but the words wouldn't come out. Because she was right. "You have me figured out?"

"Some, but you hold so much back. I figure that part of it is because you were constantly moving as a child. I can't even imagine what that would be like. I derive so much from Hope and its people. But I also think there's more behind it. Has it ever bothered you that you don't have the time to really get to know people?"

"I've learned to accept it. Every job has trade-offs. Mine is that I travel and live in different places for a short amount of time."

"No regrets?"

Again he couldn't tell her no. "I met a woman— Beth—in my second assignment with the organization. I loved her, and I thought she loved me.

We'd talked a little about marrying, but when it was time for me to leave, she didn't want to go yet. We decided to try a long-distance relationship. I flew to see her. She flew to see me. But it wasn't long before there was more and more time between our visits. The phone calls and emails weren't enough. She met another man and broke it off with me."

"And you still love her?"

"No, but I realized that a lot of women wouldn't make the commitment I did and that I couldn't ask them to give up their life to follow me."

"So it's easier just not to get involved in the first place?"

He looked her straight in her eye and said, "Yes. Why invite getting hurt?"

"That's a pretty lonely life."

"I always have a lot of people in my life. They may change every so often, but I'm not a loner."

"You aren't? You can be alone in the middle of a crowd. It's the way you approach life and others."

Alone in the middle of a crowd. He'd felt that way many times and had merely shaken it off. Lately that had become harder to do. Was that why he wanted Hannah to leave with him? Because with his sister he wouldn't be so alone? Why did he need more now? He rose and held out his hand. "I'll take your trash. I'm grabbing a brownie. Do you want one?"

"Yes." She balled her paper napkin and aluminum foil together and handed it to him.

Part of him didn't want to return to Maggie. She was challenging the way he lived. The fact that her questions had made him uncomfortable concerned him. After Beth, he'd never had trouble until he'd come to Hope. Somewhere along the way he'd opened the door to Maggie, and she was now demanding total entry.

When he sat back down under the magnolia tree and gave her a brownie, he asked, "Since I've answered your questions, I have some for you. It's obvious we look at life differently. Why are you afraid to take a risk?"

"I take risks. Granted I haven't gone skydiving or climbing Mount Everest, but I'm not afraid to do something risky."

"Are you sure about that? I'm not talking physically but emotionally. You've never considered leaving Hope and starting over somewhere else, have you?"

"No. Why would I? I'm happy here."

"Have you had any serious relationships since your fiancé was killed?"

Her gaze slanted toward the branches above her, her mouth twisting. "I've dated."

"Seriously?"

"Define seriously."

"Fallen in love, gone out with the same person for months."

She lowered her eyes and played with tearing off bits of the brownie then popping them into her mouth. "No."

He hesitated for a moment, then asked what he'd wondered for the past month. "So you're still in love with your deceased fiancé?"

Her head snapped up. "No. I'll always care about him, but he chose to re-up. I didn't want him to, but he did. I know he never thought he'd go overseas so quickly or be put into a dangerous situation where he would be killed. It was peacetime. I still remember the utter shock for months afterward and then again when Brady was born."

"If you don't love him, then why didn't you find someone else? It's been over thirteen years. Any man would be lucky to have you as a wife."

"Because it hurt. You know when a person gets burned, they stay away from the fire."

"Exactly. You and I aren't that different."

"Two wounded souls coping the best way we can?"

He nodded.

Silence descended between them. A heaviness in his chest pressed on his lungs, making each breath difficult. Hannah was about all that was

important in his life. He'd lost everyone else—
his mother, father, Beth, even the opportunity to
have good friends who would be there for him.
What was he going to do if his sister stayed here
and had her twins? Made Hope her home? Why
was he suddenly panicked about that? She'd been
living in Los Angeles, but she'd come to visit him
from time to time. With two babies that wouldn't
be an easy option. Which left him coming here
to see her.

Tension held a grip on his shoulders. He rolled
them, trying to ease the ache. It didn't help.

Maggie finished her brownie while his lay un-
touched in his palm. "Are you going to eat that?"

"I'm fuller than I thought. Want it?"

"I never let good chocolate go to waste." She
plucked it from his hand and bit into it. "Where
do you need me to help?"

"The outside is finished so we're moving inside. You can help me hang drywall."

"You know how?"

"I got a quick lesson from Zane this morning
plus he'll be in the same room."

"Aah, a safety net."

"Hannah is the handyman—woman—in the
Weston family." He panned the churchyard and
glimpsed his sister talking with Brady and pat-
ting Sadie. "She has a soft spot for animals like
Brady, but like me she's never had much of an

opportunity to have a pet. Aaron didn't like animals. Wouldn't let her have any around."

"That's a red flag to me."

"But when you're young and in love, you don't want to hear that."

"Sometimes you have to find out the hard way."

"That's life." He rose and offered her his hand, then tugged her up.

At the end of the day, hot and tired, Maggie left the new addition, the smell of sawdust, mud for the drywalls and sweat underscoring the work the group had done that hot, August day. When Cody strolled outside, he made a beeline for his car. Popping the trunk, he hauled out large plastic water guns, filled and ready to go, and began passing them out to the teens.

Immediately a war erupted, with kids running and shooting their toy weapons. Laughter echoed through the churchyard. Brady dove for cover behind a live oak tree while aiming at his friends hiding around him. Maggie jogged toward Cody, dodging a stream of water coming her way. But seconds later she got blasted by Brady.

"Bull's-eye," her son shouted.

She used Cody's car to block the next spray. "Have an extra one?"

"I brought one for everybody with a few extras for the adults." He handed her a bright pink plastic gun with a large canister to hold her ammo—water.

"Good. I have a son to pay back."

The next fifteen minutes the battle raged. Everyone ended up drenched, especially the adults when some of the youth group teamed up to go after them. Water dripping from her, Maggie shoved her wet hair out of her eyes and lined up probably her last shot—right in Cody's face. She noticed he'd run out of ammo. When she squeezed the trigger and a stream deluged him, he dropped his weapon, charged her and tackled her to the soft grass behind her. Somehow he managed to cushion her fall. He wrestled her gun away from her and jumped up, then got off a couple direct hits right in her face.

She laughed, rolling away from the downpour. "You won. You won."

"I can't believe you turned on your team."

"I thought it was every man for himself at the end." She scrambled to her feet as the gun in his hand finally dripped its last drop of water.

"Remind me not to be on your team until you understand the concept of what a team is," he said but a twinkle lit his eyes.

"Oh, I do. I just couldn't resist that last shot.

The surprise was priceless." She looked around the churchyard.

Everyone's ammo was depleted. Everyone was soaking wet. And everyone was smiling, chattering with each other. The perfect ending for a great day.

"What made you think of a water gun fight?"

"Have you ever been in a car with a bunch of sweaty guys? Since some are riding back with me, I thought this would make it less pungent in the car."

"Yeah, but now you're gonna have a bunch of wet guys riding back with you."

"Leather seats. No problem."

"Aah, then you won't mind bringing Brady home. Cloth seats."

"What are you going to do? Drive standing up?"

"I see Kim is going home with Zane. I'll just borrow one of Zane's plastic sheets to cover the front seat for Hannah and me. I'll pick up Brady at your apartment."

After everyone dried off the best they could, Maggie climbed into her vehicle with Hannah slipping into the front passenger seat. Cody's sister laid her head back against the cushion, her eyes closing.

"Having fun is a lot of hard work. The kids

did great." Hannah released a long breath. "But I don't think I have any energy left."

"Me, neither, but I'm so glad they had a good time, even Brady."

"He was trying to talk me into getting a dog from Nathan. He's a mighty persuasive kid. I can't right now. I don't know where I'll be or my circumstances with my babies, but the first time I can, I'll see Nathan."

"I'll let Brady know he was successful talking you into having a dog." Maggie turned onto the highway that led back to Hope. "So you don't know yet if you are staying or going with Cody?"

"Before, I would dive into a big decision without much thought. I'm not going to do that this time. I have more than myself to consider." Hannah angled toward Maggie. "I called Aaron this morning to talk to him. I had to leave a message. I almost didn't. I had prepared myself to talk with him, and when he wasn't there, it threw me off."

"Then you've done what you can. It's now up to him to call back."

"There's a part of me that wants him to call back. And a part that doesn't. What if he has finally decided to be a father to these babies?"

"Isn't that a good thing?"

"Honestly, no. I've seen the type of father Zane

and Gideon are. Aaron wouldn't be what my babies need."

"Are you prepared to do it all alone? Be both mother and father?"

"That's what I have to decide. Cody will do what he can as their uncle, but if I stay and he leaves, that will only be occasionally. How did you do it?"

"I had others to help me."

"What's that saying—it takes a village to raise a child?"

"So true."

The rest of the trip Hannah told Maggie about the hotel she was working on in Biloxi. It was half an hour later when Maggie pulled into the parking space in front of Cody's apartment.

"I think I'll wait out here." She pointed to her cutoffs and baggy T-shirt. "These might dry some more."

"C'mon in. Wait out on the balcony. I've gotten a hankering for some sweet tea. The first thing I have mastered making here in Hope."

"Watch out. You might turn into a Southern belle."

"Not me. I'm an electrician who is more comfortable around men than women. My mom died when I was young so it was Cody and Dad who mostly raised me."

"My mother was around, but there was always a distance between us. I never seemed to live up to what she wanted as a daughter. In the end she turned away from me when I got pregnant."

Hannah stopped in the entrance into the kitchen. "She was around and didn't help you?"

"No. The only time she saw Brady was at family functions, and a few years after he was born, she and Dad moved to Sedona. I sometimes wonder if it was because she felt uncomfortable with Brady and me around."

"What about your dad? How did he feel?"

"He basically went along with Mom's wishes. I've heard from him occasionally through the years since they left Hope. More so since she died."

"Have you thought of going to see him?"

"Yes, especially since the hurricane, but there is so much to do here. I don't know when I could do it. And I'm not sure he would want to see me. We've never talked about that."

"Maybe you should." Hannah's eyes grew round. "I probably shouldn't have said that. I'm beginning to sound like Cody. I've heard him say enough times that we have to face our problems and deal with them. They don't go away. They hide and come back to bite us when we least expect them to."

"He says that? Does he take his own advice?"

Hannah shrugged. "My big brother always seems in control so I assume he does. Let me get us something to drink."

Maggie went out on the balcony while Hannah fixed them a glass of sweet tea. Sitting in a lawn chair, she could see the parking lot from between the slats in the black iron railing. She didn't think Cody had taken his own advice, not after hearing about Beth today. She had glimpsed the hurt he'd experienced when that relationship had fallen apart. Just a glimmer as he'd talked about her, but it had been there.

Maybe somehow she could help him with it. Someone needed to look out for the person who saw to everyone else's problems.

When Cody's car stopped in the place next to hers, she started to rise to tell Hannah she wasn't going to stay after all, but when Cody and Brady didn't get out of the vehicle, she sat back down. Through the windshield, she saw her son face Cody, smiling and gesturing as if he was excited.

"I had a great time today. I can't believe you brought water guns. I've heard some talk about paintball. That was kinda like playing that." A grin spread across Brady's mouth.

"Not as painful. Those paint balls can hurt

when they hit you." Switching off his car, Cody relaxed back in the driver's seat, a good kind of tired pervading his body. He needed to do more of those type of activities. In the past when he would attend a church in a disaster area, he'd never gotten that involved, other than worshipping.

"You've played?"

"Yes. In college my friends and I often did on Saturday afternoons. That's when my admiration for our servicemen grew."

"My dad was in the army. He died on a mission."

"My father was in the service, too. For over twenty years."

"He was?"

"I moved from base to base. Once or twice we barely unpacked and had to turn around and leave again." Cody could remember getting rid of some of his personal items because it was a pain to pack them all the time.

"I'd like to travel. One of my friends goes on a vacation every summer. I get jealous when he brings back tons of pictures of places I would like to see."

"You'll have time."

"Yeah, when I grow up. Mom's said that to me

before. I don't think she'll ever leave here. New Orleans, Jackson and Mobile are about it for her."

A bark from Sadie, wedged between Cody and Brady, demanded their attention.

"I haven't forgotten about you, girl." Brady scratched her behind her ears.

"She sure has taken to you."

"Yeah, I understand her."

"Why do you say that?"

"I know what it's like to have everything in your life disturbed, unsure. She needs to feel loved, that I'll be here for her."

Turning toward the boy, Cody draped one arm over the steering wheel. "Everyone needs that."

"I know Mom loves me, but how do you not get scared when everything changes so quickly?"

"That's a good question. I try to keep my focus on the Lord. He's my strength when I need some. Sorta like Sadie turning to you. She's finding you're her strength."

"I am?"

"Who does she come to all the time? You. You're giving her the stability she needs after what she went through. Stability comes from within, Brady. It isn't a house or a physical object. All that can be rebuilt like we did at the church today."

Brady stared out the windshield while petting his dog. "So you're never scared?"

"I didn't say that. I get scared just like you. That's going to happen. It's what happens after it that's important. How you deal with the change, the fear."

"Have you ever been through a hurricane?"

"No. But I have been in a tornado when my family lived in Oklahoma. We were living in what people called tornado alley. That spring there were two that struck near us." One of them took his mother. "I know what fear is." And deep sadness and guilt. His mother wouldn't be dead if she hadn't been coming after him.

Brady lifted Sadie and nuzzled his face against her side. "I don't want to go through another hurricane. We were holed up about an hour north of here, and it was bad there. Uncle Keith wouldn't leave so Kim stayed while Mom took Anna and me to Hattiesburg. We didn't sleep the whole night as the storm blew. Mom worried about Uncle Keith and Kim. She had a hard time keeping Anna calm. I had to act brave. But I wasn't brave inside."

"And neither was I when the tornados came through my area."

"Is that why you try to help people after bad things happen?"

"Yes. I know what they're going through." Cody didn't like to relive that last tornado that took his mother, but each time he used that experience to help someone else the pain of his loss eased for a while. Then the guilt would return—every time he let thoughts of his mother into his mind.

"I guess that's your apartment up there." Brady nodded toward the balcony where Maggie and Hannah, glasses in hand, peered down at the car.

"Yep."

Brady pushed open the car door while carrying Sadie. "Wait till Mom hears I get to keep my water gun."

Cody chuckled. The moment of connecting with Brady was over, but they were taking small steps forward at least. "I'm not sure she's going to be as thrilled as you are."

"Wise of Mom. She may never be safe out in the garden again."

Cody exited the car with Sadie's cart in tow. "Just wait to use it when I'm not around." When he said that and thought about leaving Hope for his next assignment, a few seconds of dread chilled him in the hot sun.

Chapter Ten

"Is Hannah there?" Cody asked the second Maggie came on the phone Sunday afternoon.

The urgency in his voice alerted her that something was wrong. "No. What happened?" She checked outside the kitchen window to make sure his sister hadn't come.

"She called Aaron. I left the room, not wanting to eavesdrop on her conversation. Now I wish I had. The next thing I heard was the front door slamming closed. When I went outside, I saw her getting into her car, crying. Her tires actually screeched when she drove out of the parking lot. By the time I got my keys and ran to my car, she was gone. I didn't see which way she went. I was hoping she was at your place."

"I wish she was." She walked into the dining room and peered out that window. Nothing. "She told me she called him yesterday and left a message. I thought she was going to wait until he called her back."

"When we came home from church, she was quiet. Didn't say anything at lunch either even when I tried to get her to talk. I knew something was bothering her, but she wouldn't say anything to me. That's why I thought she might have come over to talk to you."

"Sorry. Any other idea where she might have gone?"

"No. I'm just going to drive around. Maybe I'll find her."

"I'll help. I'll drive around this part of town and you take the west end. I'll call you if I find her."

"Thanks. I'll do the same."

Maggie grabbed her purse and headed for her car. She tried to think of a place Hannah would go. She went to Broussard Park and walked out to the lighthouse. A couple families had gathered at the picnic area even though it was over ninety degrees and humid. Some teens were shooting baskets on the court. Kids were climbing the equipment on the playground. She even looked toward Hope Community Church. But there was no sign of Hannah or the used car she'd bought.

When Maggie got back into her Dodge, she replayed the conversations she'd had with Hannah lately. Yesterday she'd been talking about the hotel and the pier that ran along one side of it. Hannah had commented how much she liked to go out there at lunch and eat her sandwich.

She called Cody. "Have you found her?"

"No, and I'm running out of places to look."

"I'm going to the hotel she's working on in Biloxi. I know it's a long shot, but we were talking about it yesterday."

"Fine. I've got a couple more areas left." Tension roughened his voice. "If you find her, call and I'll come."

Thirty minutes later Maggie parked at the end of the pier next to the hotel under construction—beside Hannah's car. Once she spied Hannah herself out on the pier she called Cody.

"I found her at the hotel pier where she's working."

"I'm on my way."

"Let me talk to her. Go home. I'll either call you to come or I'll bring her home." When that suggestion was met with silence, she continued. "I know what's happening to her. I can relate."

"Okay." The word was drawn out as if it had been difficult to say.

As Maggie strolled toward Cody's sister, Hannah faced the sea, the breeze whipping her long blond hair about her face. Her posture, hunched over the railing, conveyed a woman struggling with her emotions.

"Hannah, are you all right?"

Hannah's shoulders rose and fell. Her hands dropped from the railing and flexed at her sides. Slowly she rotated toward Maggie. "He accused me of trying to trap him into a marriage. Told me there was no way he was going to be forced to marry me. That was before I could say more than 'Hello, this is Hannah.'" Her eyes gleamed with unshed tears.

"I'm sorry. Didn't you tell me y'all were talking about getting married?"

"Yes. Not right away but in a year or so when we both had better jobs and could save some money."

"Then what he says doesn't make sense. He'd been planning to marry you anyway."

"Maybe. Maybe it was all talk." A wet track ran down her cheek, and Hannah brushed it away.

"Why did you call him? I thought you were going to wait for him to call you."

"After listening to your pastor talk today about letting go of hurts in the past, I'd wanted to tell Aaron I understood he had been scared when I broke the news to him. I still wanted him to be in his kids' lives, even if he didn't want to marry me. I didn't want them to miss out on having a dad."

"Did you tell him that?"

"No, he hung up on me before I got the chance. I'm not calling him back. I've done all I can. It's just that—that…" The tears returned to stream down Hannah's face.

"What?"

Hannah sniffled and wiped her eyes. "I want my kids to grow up with a father. At least I had one, even if he was gone a lot. I'd wished he was around more, but I knew when he returned, he'd always do what he could for me. I don't want my kids to have a hole in their lives even before they're born."

"Is that the way you felt?"

"Sometimes. I don't want to go with Cody, traveling from place to place, but with my brother, at least my boys would have a man in their life."

"You're having boys? Why didn't you tell me yesterday?"

"I was still trying to get used to the news the doctor told me Friday. For months I'd been dreaming I was going to have girls. I'd talked myself into believing I could handle girls by myself because I know how females think. Now I'm not sure. I hated sports in school. I was never a tomboy even if I became an electrician. How am I going to do all of that for not one but two sons?"

Maggie put her arm around Hannah. "C'mon. Let's head back to Hope. We'll leave your car here and I'll tell you about a few of my same worries when Brady was born."

"I'm sorry you came all the way over here. I know Cody worries about me. Probably for good reason. Lately I've been crying all the time."

"Welcome to the world of being pregnant. I could tell you stories about that, too."

By the time Maggie pulled up to Cody's apartment, Hannah had laughed, shared a little more about Aaron's treatment of her and her dilemma concerning her brother. She wanted to stand on her own two feet but also realized the huge change about to occur in her life with the birth of her twins.

"Thanks for listening to me, Maggie. I think with all that is happening the worst part is that I can't decide what to do. I don't know what is best. I have such a strong urge to stay here, but…" Hannah looked out the windshield and swallowed hard.

Maggie removed the key from the ignition. "You don't have to decide right now. Give it time. The right answer will come to you. Pray about it. If you decide to go with Cody, you can always change your mind and return. I promise I won't forget you." *Nor your brother.*

"That's true. I don't see Zane's work slowing down anytime soon." Hannah looked up at Cody's apartment. "I guess we'd better go let Cody know I'm all right."

"I'm surprised he isn't out here."

As Maggie mounted the stairs with Hannah to the apartment, Cody opened the door, his eyes soft with concern. "We decided to ride back together. Your sister will need a lift to work tomorrow." She followed Hannah inside, wanting to make sure the young woman was truly all right.

Near the hallway to the bedrooms, Hannah swung around. "I'm tired. I'm gonna lie down. Thanks, Maggie, for making me feel like a normal pregnant woman." She gave Maggie a quick hug then disappeared down the corridor.

"A normal pregnant woman?" Cody murmured behind her, only a foot away.

His husky voice, laced with a trace of humor, sent goose bumps spreading down her body. "You know all those hormones rampaging through us, making us cry at the slightest thing."

"Ah, *that* 'normal.' I'm glad this is only temporary."

"You and thousands of other men."

His chuckle tingled along her neck as he moved

past her into the living room. "Would you like some sweet tea? I know how much you love it."

"No, but we should talk."

He turned toward her. "Thanks for helping Hannah. Frankly I wasn't sure what to say to her. I'm not real rational when talking about Aaron with her. If I ever see him…" He waved his hand toward the couch. "Never mind. I don't think we'll see him anytime soon."

"I don't think so, either. He made it clear to her that he didn't want to have anything to do with her or his children."

"Legally he may not have a choice."

"True, and Hannah and I talked about that on the way home. She doesn't want to pursue financial support from Aaron. She's determined somehow to make it on her own. By the end of the ride, she'd decided her sons will be better off without him in their lives—even a little."

"Sons? Is that what the doctor told her Friday?"

Hannah nodded. "I thought she had told you."

"I didn't realize she would find out on Friday. The last time she went they couldn't tell." The corners of his mouth lifted into a grin that reached deep into his eyes. "Two nephews. I like that. I wasn't sure about what to do with girls. But boys I know a thing or two about."

"It has Hannah a little nervous. The way you feel about girls is the way she feels about boys."

"That's okay. I'll help her." He sat beside her on the couch, facing her, his arm along the back cushion. "But why didn't she say anything to me Friday night?" The grin dimmed, his eyebrows crunching together.

"I think probably because she still doesn't know what she wants to do when you need to leave."

"This should cinch it. Her sons need a male in their lives. It won't be their father but I'm perfect. Uncle Cody. I like the sound of that. Maybe I can pass along what I'm learning from Brady about fishing. I never thought I would get into it, but I've been enjoying myself."

"I'm glad you are. Brady seems to be, too. But I need to point out there are a lot of girls who like to fish, too. You could do that with nieces as well as nephews. I'm telling you because the doctor couldn't tell on the second baby for sure. He was hiding behind his brother."

"But you think it's a boy."

"I'm only saying that because probably it is unless they aren't identical twins."

As if he dismissed that possibility, Cody mused aloud, "Two boys. I'm liking that more and more.

I also played football. I could get them involved in that, too."

Laughing, she took his hand to get his full attention. "I suggest you quit planning your nephews' childhoods. Hannah may have her own opinion. You've already got them fishing and playing football. When are they going to play with friends, study?"

The light in his eyes brightened. "After guitar lessons." A smile curled the corners of his mouth. "I had dreams as a teen of being a rock star. They didn't last long, but putting together a band while I was living in Biloxi my sophomore year was fun. I wonder what happened to it. I had to leave a few weeks before we were going to perform at our first party."

"You didn't keep up with any of them?"

"No. I found a clean break was easier when leaving a town."

The matter-of-fact way he said that last sentence sliced through her heart. Today it was so easy to keep up with people even half a world away. She didn't want him to walk out of her life and not ever hear from him again. Her hand slipped from his, and she leaned back, putting more space between them.

Maggie rose. "I'd better go. I left without telling anyone where I was. Not that I have to, but they may begin to wonder if I'm going to fix dinner tonight."

"Before she'd left, we had decided I was grilling steaks tonight while Hannah made a salad and baked a couple potatoes. Not particularly difficult." In one fluid motion, he was on his feet and closing the gap between them. "Thank you for helping me. When Hannah starts crying, I don't know what to say to her. The other day I found her sobbing at a commercial on TV."

"Some of them are tearjerkers."

"This wasn't. It was about buying a certain dog food."

"But remember she'd like to have a pet. That might have been what was behind it." She backed away a few steps before she surrendered to her desires and invited herself to dinner.

"Do you have to fix dinner tonight? I can get another steak thawed pretty fast."

"Yes," she said so quickly it even surprised her.

Cody blinked several times. "I know that was last minute, but…"

The creases on his forehead enticed her to smooth them away. She clenched her hands so tightly, her nails stabbed her palms. "I'd love to some other time. You've got your dinner planned and so do I." Another pace back and she could breathe a little easier. Her heartbeat calmed—slightly.

Unfortunately her hen was still in the freezer. She checked her watch and winced. She might have to rethink dinner, but the one thing she was sure about was that she couldn't spend the evening with Cody. She was beginning to see why he cut all ties when he left. There was some wisdom in that method.

As she moved toward the exit, he mirrored her steps. It just wasn't fair. How was she supposed to keep her distance when he kept breaching her personal space?

As she reached for the door, he leaned against it, effectively stopping her from opening it and fleeing down the stairs. His shoulder cushioning against her escape route, he loosely folded his arms over his chest. "How about a steak dinner next weekend? No last-minute plans."

A date? No. Yes. "Let me check my calendar. I never know with Brady what's going on." The statement even sounded lame to her. Her son hadn't done much of anything this summer so why was next weekend any different?

"Fine. Just let me know. I'm flexible."

I'm flustered. "Okay. I'll talk to you this week at City Hall." She put her hand on the knob to turn it.

But he still lounged against the door. When he covered her hand and tugged her toward him, she was in deep trouble. Her heartbeat increased its tempo, pounded against her rib cage. Its pulsating throb thundered through her head. Hannah probably heard it and would be in here any second to interrupt what Maggie knew was coming next.

A kiss.

When his lips touched hers softly, she nearly sank to the floor. She clutched his arms and gave into the sensations he produced in her. He wrapped her in his embrace and deepened the kiss. Her lungs deprived of air, she finally turned her head slightly.

He trailed light brushes of his lips against her skin from her mouth to her ear. "I wish you would stay for dinner." The huskiness of his voice attested to her effect on him.

Finally a hint of sanity returned to her. She gently pushed back, grasped the knob and wrenched open the door before she changed her mind. "I'll see you this week."

She made it outside and drank in the hot, stifling air to fill her oxygen-starved lungs. Sensing him watching her, she kept moving down the stairs and somehow slid behind her steering wheel. She gripped it as if that would orient her to her surroundings. But it didn't. Closing her eyes, she saw in her mind, Cody's mouth coming toward hers. Her lips had tingled in anticipation, and when they had connected with his, she hadn't been disappointed.

It's too late to avoid it. I'm falling in love with him, and when he leaves, I'll be hurt. Badly.

"You were so quiet during dinner. Are you all right?" Kim asked as she helped Maggie clear the table while the rest of the family went into the den.

"No, everything is wrong."

"Aah, Ruth told me you were over at Cody's earlier. What happened?"

"He kissed me again."

"And that's a bad thing? I thought you liked him."

"I do—too much." Maggie placed the dishes in the sink.

"What's wrong with that? It's about time you got serious again. Dedicating yourself to the memory of your deceased fiancé is admirable, but enough is enough. Go out and live your life."

"Did anyone ever tell you that you're blunt?"

"Zane, just this morning."

"It figures." Maggie rinsed off a plate and handed it to Kim to put in the dishwasher. "I need a man who will stay around. In case you didn't realize, Cody isn't. He should be leaving in the next month."

"So? What's stopping you from leaving Hope?"

"I don't want to."

"Then, Maggie, something else is going on here because when you fall in love, it doesn't make any difference where the two of you are. You should be able to find a way for it to work if you're meant to be together."

"I should never talk to a newlywed," Maggie mumbled, having heard the same from Ruth. She was surrounded by happily married women. Didn't anyone understand? Her life would be totally changed. Brady's would be, too. How could—

Ruth came into the kitchen, a frown carved into her features. "I heard on the news there's a hurricane in the Gulf heading this way. Hurricane Carl."

Chapter Eleven

The glass Maggie held nearly slipped from her wet fingers. Another hurricane coming toward them. No! They were still recovering from the last one. "How far away is it?"

"It's heading for the western part of Cuba on a northwesterly path. It's picking up speed."

"Does Brady know?"

"Yes. The kids had the TV on and, during the commercial break, the weatherman talked about the quickly developing storm."

"What are the winds right now?" Kim took the glass from Maggie.

"Ninety miles per hour."

"Okay, we can deal with this. We have to remain calm. Brady and Anna don't need to see our fear," Maggie said in a voice surprisingly calm while inside turmoil ruled, churning her stomach like a hurricane-tossed sea.

"I know one thing. We'll all leave this time. And if Keith refuses, I'll have Zane and Gideon tie him up and stick him in the car." Ruth twisted her hands together. "But don't tell Keith that. I just know he's not going to ride this storm out like he did Naomi."

"I don't think Dad will, not after seeing how close he came to dying last time. But, Maggie, you're right. We've got to keep it together. We have some time to plan. It could be four days away. We have…" Kim's voice faded into silence as Brady and Anna appeared in the doorway behind Ruth.

The boy's pale face mirrored the fear in Anna's. "Mom, what are we gonna do?"

Maggie crossed the room and settled her hand on Brady's left shoulder. "As Aunt Kim said, we're going to plan and wait. It's too far away to tell where the hurricane will go for sure. If it comes this way, we'll be all right."

"We weren't last time, and now I have Sadie to take care of. I don't want anything like last time happening to her."

Maggie placed her other hand on his right shoulder and waited until she had his full attention. "*We* will take care of Sadie. We learned a lot with Hurricane Naomi. We can use that to our advantage."

Brady dropped his gaze to the floor. Sadie nudged him. He scooped her up and cradled her next to his chest. "Can you stop it from destroying our town a second time?" He spun around and hurried down the hall to the stairs.

The sound of his footsteps as he stomped upstairs echoed through the house. The past couple weeks her son had been responding to his sessions with Cody. Had that all been destroyed in a matter of minutes?

The thought weighed her down. While Ruth, Anna and Kim talked behind her, she trudged up to the second floor. Each time she lifted her foot, it felt as though she had a block of cement around it.

She knocked on Brady's door and waited for him to let her in. When he didn't, she turned the knob and went into his bedroom. He stood at the window that looked toward the Gulf with Sadie still clutched to him.

"I went to the beach today with Sadie after church, and the water was so calm. Deceiving us into thinking everything was going to be okay. It's not. Even if we leave, what are we going to come back to? A home destroyed totally this time?"

The questions her son was asking were ones that had been sounding through her mind since

Ruth had made the announcement. She didn't have an answer for him. "Whatever happens we will face it together." Her reply seemed lacking even to her. More like a platitude, not a real solution.

"You don't have to babysit me. I've got Sadie."

His words dismissed her, but she remained rooted to the floor.

He pivoted. "Really, Mom, I don't feel like talking."

He didn't yell at her. Instead he spoke as though he was tired of fighting and was giving up.

"Brady, we don't know if the hurricane will affect us."

"Yeah, sure." He placed Sadie on his bed then strode to Maggie and guided her to the door.

Before she knew it, she was in the hall—shut out of her son's room. She started to go back in and demand he talk with her. But then that hadn't worked well lately. She made her way to the game room's back door that led to the second-floor gallery.

Outside, a gentle breeze cooled the hot August evening. In the distance a nearly full moon burned bright in a clear sky. If she could see the water across the highway, she imagined it was still calm. Hurricane Carl was days away.

She turned from the railing and glimpsed her

son on his bed, staring at the ceiling, Sadie lying by his side, her head resting on his stomach. He needed to talk to someone. If not her, then Cody.

Taking out her cell, she placed a call to Cody. "There's another hurricane out in the Gulf, heading this way if it stays on course."

"Ruth just called me. She figured I needed to know because of the clients I work with. Does Brady know?"

"Yes, and right now he's on his bed, staring at the ceiling. He won't talk to me about it, but he's clearly upset. I'm worried."

"I'll come over. Maybe he'll talk to me."

"I hope so."

Maggie clicked off but the words she longed to say to Cody remained locked inside of her. *Talk to me too and tell me everything will be okay.* After Hurricane Naomi had hit at the end of October last year, she'd felt battered and bruised emotionally. Lately she'd begun to think she was finally piecing everything back together. Now it was for nothing. She would have to start all over.

Sinking down onto one of the lounge chairs on the second-floor gallery, she thought of what they would have to do to ready the house for another storm—mere weeks after it had been repaired after the last one. Some of the storm shutters weren't up yet. They would have to be installed or boards purchased to cover those windows. Everything outside would have to be brought inside. Supplies bought in case the power went out. The list grew longer the more she thought about preparing for Hurricane Carl.

Overwhelmed, she laid her head against the back cushion and closed her eyes. Her mind went blank.

Sometime later, the sound of a car coming down the drive drew her attention. Cody. As it pulled around to the back of the house, she shoved to her feet and moved to the stairs to wait for him. She followed his progress up the steps. Although his face was in the shadows, she felt his gaze on her, reading her. She moved away from the stream of light from inside. Tears stung her eyes, but she would not cry in front of him.

He stopped near her, taking her hands. "How are you doing?"

"Peachy. I'm looking forward to going through another storm." Defeat laced each word, and she hated that. But that didn't change how she felt. "Sorry. You don't need to hear that." She tugged her hands free from his.

"Is it the truth?"

"Yes."

"Then I want to hear it. I imagine I'll hear it a lot in the next few days."

"What are you going to say to those people?"

He sighed. "I could tell you it will depend on the person, which it will. But mostly I want the people to feel they do have control over how they respond to the news. They may not be able to control if the hurricane comes or not, but their reaction and what they do about the storm are in their hands."

"That sounds so easy. It's not all the time."

"I know. I've been there." He paused, then said, "I lost my mother to a tornado. And our home was severely damaged."

"You never told me that."

"It's not something I talk about much. I was a child when it happened. Near Brady's age. It really has no bearing on what's happening now." His jaw clenched into a hard line.

"Are you sure? This time if the hurricane strikes, you won't be going to a disaster after the fact but be in the middle of one occurring."

"It doesn't change anything. It just means I'll be able to help others right away." He tensed, his gaze sliding away from her.

He wasn't telling her something. He could tell her it didn't make any difference, but his body language said otherwise. "I guess you're right because Hope isn't really your home. You don't have anything at stake here like the rest of us."

He flinched and stepped back until he bumped into the railing behind him. "Keeping myself detached helps me cope. I found that out the first year on the job. I throw all my emotional energy into helping others. I don't have time to shore myself up because I become so invested in my clients."

"How long do most of the counselors last with Christian Assistance Coalition?"

"Maybe five years."

"And you?"

"Seven."

"How many vacations have you had over those years?"

"Three."

"You worry about me taking care of myself. I worry about you."

"Don't. This is my job," he said in a voice drenched with tension. Then he looked around. "Where's Brady? I'm sure I'll get other calls tonight."

Hope wouldn't be the only town affected. There would always be a disaster occurring somewhere in the world. To have someone like Cody who understood what it was like to go through one was important for the survivors. She couldn't deny that. "Brady's in his bedroom. I'll be out here after you talk with him."

When he went into the house, Maggie began pacing. She couldn't sit. Restlessness zipped through her. She circled the second-floor gallery. Passing by Brady's window, she caught sight of Cody sitting at the foot of her son's bed, Brady leaning against the headboard. She slowed and watched as Brady said something, a scowl on his face.

She forced herself away from the window and continued her trek around the perimeter of the house. The next time she walked past her son's window, she spied him holding Sadie on his lap, stroking her while intent on what Cody was saying. When she reached the back stairs across from the door into the game room, she stopped and perched herself against the railing to wait for Cody.

Closing her eyes, she listened to an owl hoot in a tree at the back of the property. The scent of the sea saturated the air, with the fragrance of a couple gardenia bushes below vying for dominance. She imagined waves rhythmically washing up on the shore not far away—the sound soothing, lulling her into a sense of peace. If only she could feel that way. If only she didn't feel her life was falling apart all over again like right after she found out Robbie had died in the line of fire.

The door opened. She straightened as Cody

crossed to her, his expression even, offering no indication of what had transpired with Brady. She waited for him to break the silence.

"He's upset but we talked about what he could do if Hurricane Carl hits Hope. What he can control. Where he can make a difference. We're going gigging for flounders again tomorrow night. That is if the water isn't too rough by then. If not, we can sit at the end of a pier and fish."

In other words, he would have another session with Brady. "Thanks. I've been worried about him."

"I've been worried about you."

"You don't have to be. I'm fine." Her declaration rushed from her before she really thought about what she said.

He cradled her chin. "Are you?"

Her throat thickened. She swallowed several times, but the tears demanded release. *No, I've got to be strong. I'm always the calm one.* She rotated toward the railing, clutching it, her fingernails digging into the wood that had been replaced since the last hurricane. Would it have to be again?

Cody came up beside her, his arm inches from hers. "You know what I think. You have been so busy making sure everyone else is all right that you have forgotten to take care of yourself. For

the past nine months, you've held this family together. Actually for the last thirteen years, you've
been there for Brady and later for your uncle.
You keep the house clean. You usually prepare
the meals. You listen to others. Knit shawls for
women who need a little extra comfort. Maybe
it's time for you to look out for yourself. It's okay
every once in a while to do that."

His words washed over her like the waves on
the beach, luring her toward that peace she cherished. She could see it just up ahead. But it flick-
ered and went out like a neon sign of welcome in
the dark of night going black.

She pried her fingers from the railing and
moved away from Cody. "You're telling me this
when your work is to look after others. To help
them overcome their problems."

"Yes, but I take time for myself."

"Do you? Besides going fishing with Brady,
which isn't really for pleasure since you're counseling him, what have you done for yourself since
you've arrived in Hope?"

"I went out on Zane's boat on the Fourth of
July. I read your romance."

"Before that."

"I read in the evening when I could. Jogged
some." He let out a rough breath. "This isn't a
conversation about who takes time for leisure

activities. This is about addressing what you feel regarding a problem rather than suppressing it. That may work for a while, but in the long run it will come out."

"What do you want me to say? That I'm tired? I am. That I'm angry this is happening again to Hope? I am." Her voice caught on the last word as tears flooded her eyes, Cody's image shimmering before her. "This has been a long day. I can't have this conversation anymore. Good night."

He reached out to touch her. She evaded his hand and backed away, one tear leaking from her eye and rolling down her cheek. She whirled around and escaped inside the house. Then, like a deluge, sorrow rained down on her. Because she wanted more with Cody. But he didn't.

Cody stared at the door Maggie had closed. A barrier. It might as well be a stone wall with no way through. He wanted to help her—needed to—but for once, he didn't have anything to say to her that would make things right.

What do You want me to do, God? I don't know anymore.

Cody made his way to his car. These next few days would be difficult, and for the first time, he didn't know if he had it in him. People would depend on him to make sense of something that didn't make sense.

Why, Lord? Why Hope again?

"We haven't gotten many hits this evening," Cody said to Brady while they sat at the end of the pier, their feet dangling over the water.

"Sometimes you do. Sometimes you don't."

"It sounds like you're doing better today."

Brady lifted one shoulder in a shrug. "Not much I can do about the hurricane. Aunt Ruth told me it passed Cuba early this morning. Still heading this way. But we are doing what we can to get ready. We'll go to Hattiesburg again. Mom called her friend this morning, and she has invited us to stay with her. Sadie will be safe. She'll go with us."

Cody didn't usually track hurricanes, but he was this one. It had grown stronger with winds up to 125 miles per hour with still a lot of Gulf to go to feed its strength.

"We started storm preparation today. Zane installed the rest of the shutters with Gideon's help. I brought in all the outside stuff."

"How's your uncle Keith doing?"

"Okay, I guess. He hasn't said much."

"I thought I would drop in after we fish." He'd had to work with a lot of his clients today, helping them to deal with what was happening. He'd been surprised Keith hadn't called or come by, especially with Ruth working down the hall from him. When he'd picked up Brady, Keith had been gone to the store. He hoped he was there later.

For a few minutes, Brady remained silent, reeling in his line, checking his shrimp bait then putting it back in the water. "You know that day I told you I hated God, I didn't mean it."

"What did you mean?"

"I was angry at Him. Do you think He's upset because I was?"

"No, God loves us no matter what. It's like when you do something you shouldn't and your mom still loves you in spite of what you did."

"Yeah, Mom is like that."

"You can tell God anything. He forgives us." The words came out almost without thought. Cody had said those very words before many times, but suddenly he listened to what he was saying. Really listened. Had he ever talked with the Lord about what happened that day his mother was killed in the tornado? About his part in it?

"Cody?"

Brady saying his name snagged Cody's attention. "Yeah?"

"I'm worried about Mom. I went to her room last night to talk to her and heard her crying."

"What about?"

"Don't know. I didn't disturb her. I didn't know what to say to her."

"Do you want me to talk to her?"

Brady shifted toward him, his gaze fixed on him. "Would you?"

"If I can help, I will."

Drawing in a deep breath, the boy turned to face forward. "Good. I know you can help her."

I'm not so sure. He was too close to her. He'd made the mistake of getting too emotionally involved. It was hard for him to step back and look at Maggie objectively anymore. But he would do what he could.

"I've got a bite!" Brady scrambled to his feet and began reeling in his fish.

"We got a lot done today. We're in good shape." Maggie took her seat at the kitchen table.

"Good shape! Maybe I should take pictures of this place. In a few days it may be gone." Keith stabbed the baked chicken piece he wanted and passed the platter to Ruth.

"Uncle Keith, we have flood insurance now. We are covered a lot better than last year."

He snorted. "That's the point. It hasn't even

been a year, and we are right back where we were nine months ago."

Ruth covered his hand. "But this time we are stronger. We have each other."

Keith's gaze fastened on his wife, and the frown dissolved into a soft look. "Yeah, you're right." A moment later, he dragged his attention to Maggie. "You're right. We're in better shape than last year. Goodness knows, we have this hurricane routine down pat now."

Maggie took Uncle Keith's free hand then Ruth's and began to pray. "Lord, protect Hope from the hurricane and if it does strike the town, please keep everyone safe. We're in Your hands now. Amen."

Uncle Keith scooped up the steamed cauliflower. "Where's Brady?"

"Fishing with Cody."

"He worked hard today. I'm glad he went. It might be a while before he can fish with this storm approaching." Uncle Keith forked a piece of his chicken and cut it with a knife.

"They couldn't go gigging for flounders. The water is getting rough so they're at the pier at the end of Bayview. I sent sandwiches with Brady so he wouldn't have to rush back."

"In other words, if he needs to talk with Cody,

he has the time." Ruth sipped her drink. "I know Kathleen's boys are worried."

"So is Anna," Uncle Keith said.

Ruth frowned. "This is hard on children."

"And adults," Maggie whispered as she stared at her food, none of it appealing at the moment.

"You're always there for everyone. Are *you* okay?"

Her uncle's gruff voice, full of concern, demanded she say something. But what? The truth? He'd always counted on her to be upbeat when no one else was. She didn't have it in her now.

Maggie scooted back her chair. "I'm not hungry. Excuse me."

She heard Uncle Keith call out to her, but she continued toward the back door and left. She felt like a cheerleader who could no longer chant the team to victory. When she descended the steps, she peered at her garden, usually a haven for her. All she saw was what it had looked like after Hurricane Naomi. Destroyed totally. She'd spent months cultivating it, and it was finally starting to remind her of its former beauty. All that time wasted.

Maggie stalked around to the front of the house and stared down the long drive. The wind blew at a brisk pace. In the distance she saw the whitecaps on the water. They would increase over the next days.

When she came to the end of the driveway, she turned left toward Bayview. If she felt like this, she wondered how Brady was doing. He'd been quiet today, doing everything asked of him but without saying anything. She'd tried to engage him in a conversation about school coming up, but he'd only answered in monosyllables. As she neared the end of the pier, Cody and Brady sat side by side, the sound of her son's laughter snatched by the wind and carried to her.

Maybe she shouldn't interrupt. Why was she even here? She backpedaled and spun around to leave.

"Maggie," Cody called out her name.

She glanced over her shoulder.

He gestured for her to come join them. She headed toward them, at first slowly but as she drew closer her speed increased. The smile on their faces beckoned her. Even with the signs that bad weather was coming toward Hope, she needed to be with them. She didn't want to be alone with her thoughts right now.

"How have y'all done?" She stopped behind them and lifted the top of the cooler.

Cody answered. "Great. I caught two Spanish mackerels and several catfish. I threw those back, but Brady is the real fisherman. He's gotten three speckled trout and not one catfish."

Her son grinned as he reeled in his line. "We've got enough to fix for dinner tomorrow night." He pushed to his feet. "I'm gonna go on back and clean the fish. Can Cody come to dinner tomorrow?"

"Sure, if he wants to." Maggie glanced at Cody as he brought in his line. "How about it?"

"I'd love to." Cody took Brady's rod. "Looks like you're going to have your hands full. I'll bring back the fishing gear."

"You two can stay." Her son hefted the cooler and started toward the road.

"I get the feeling he doesn't want us to tag along with him." Staring at Brady, she saw none of the slumped shoulders and downcast eyes that had been so common only a month ago. "You must have had a good session today."

"Actually we didn't talk a lot about Hurricane Carl. We did talk about Frisky and Sadie. He's glad you brought Sadie home. Every time he sees her, he realizes his problems weren't as bad as hers."

Gripping the wooden railing, Maggie faced the Gulf. The salty scent of the air always calmed her, even when she knew what could hit Hope in a couple days. Or was it the sound of the waves rolling onto the shore? Either way, she loved coming down to Bayview Pier. To the west the sun neared the horizon, a bright orange-yellow ball reflecting its light off a few gathering clouds.

Cody put the rods on the pier next to the fishing box, then straightened and leaned against the railing. "What a day."

"One you wouldn't want to repeat?"

"Not up to six o'clock. Fishing with Brady was a treat. Before that it was...hectic."

"From what I saw, you had one person after another coming into your office, and I wasn't there nearly as long as you were. Ruth and I left to work on getting the house prepared for the storm."

"You all did a good job. The whole town has."

"How are people feeling?"

"Exactly how you would think. Scared. Angry. Frustrated. Confused. Some are feeling all of those emotions simultaneously. Brady said that Keith was quiet today. I thought I would stop by and talk with him."

"I'm sure he would love to see you, but you know I think Uncle Keith will do okay. He has Ruth now. He started to get worked up and all she did was take his hand and speak to him in a calm voice. One look at her and his blood pressure plummeted. When I watch them, I see two people deeply in love." *And I wish I had it.*

"My mother and dad were like that," Cody said. "It was the one thing that made each move bearable. They were a team. My mom made each move an adventure."

"How old were you when your mom died?"

"Twelve. Things changed drastically after that. Dad didn't know what to do without Mom. He retreated into his work. I took on more responsibility for raising Hannah."

"Did you mind?"

"No, it was my penance."

She angled toward him. "Penance? For what?"

His eyes darkened and his jaw tightened as he looked at her. "My mother was out on the road in the tornado because of me. She'd been in a car coming to pick me up and had to get out on the highway to seek shelter in a ditch. She did not make it."

Chapter Twelve

"You think you're responsible for her death?"

Cody wanted to look away but couldn't. The compassion in Maggie's expression unraveled knots of tension in his neck and shoulders. "We were moving again, and I'd just found out that morning. I got mad and decided to run away. I got about halfway across town when the clouds started getting darker and darker. I called her, and she told me to stay at the Quick and Go, that she would be there shortly." He shook his head. "She never showed up because the tornado struck." He stared at the water splashing against the pilings of the pier below him. "She would be alive today if I hadn't left home angry."

"It was an accident."

"That's what Dad kept telling me, but I heard the disappointment in his voice. He stopped short of accusing me of causing my mother's death, but I saw it in his eyes. Things between us were never the same."

"You've been carrying that around for almost twenty years?"

"Most of the time I manage not to think about it. Lately I have been a lot."

"Why?"

"Just like I've told you and everyone else. If you don't deal with the problem, it won't go away. It will need to be dealt with sooner or later. My sooner or later is now. I can't keep running from this. Your son made me see that today. I don't know how to forgive myself. Hannah grew up without a mother for most of her life because of what I did. And Dad was gone more and more after Mom died."

"Who stayed with you?"

"A housekeeper. My father was a colonel by that time and had the money to hire someone wherever we were stationed." Most were impersonal, there to do their job and no more. No one had come close to replacing his mother in his life.

"Is that why you feel Hannah needs to come with you?"

Her question surprised him. He stepped back, not sure what he felt or should say.

"You feel you owe Hannah," Maggie continued.

"She was only four when Mom died. Look at

what she missed out on." The words came without thought. He blinked and took another pace away from Maggie. "Yes, I owe her. I can't make things okay for my dad but I can for her."

"You don't think you've done enough penance for something you had no control over?"

He started to tell her no, but his cell rang. He quickly answered, glad for the interruption. "Hello."

"Dr. Weston, my mother has locked herself in her bedroom and won't come out. I can hear her crying in there." It was the daughter of Mrs. Abare, one of his clients.

He forgot his own problem and went immediately into counselor mode. "Is she upset over the hurricane?"

"She refuses to leave her home this time."

"Keep talking to her calmly. I'll be right over." He pocketed his cell. "I've got to go."

"I understand, but Cody, you need to live your own life. You have nothing to make up for. You were a kid. I can remember three years ago Brady packing a bag and telling me he was going over to a friend's house to live. I let him go and it only took a day for him to decide to return. Kids get upset with their parents and do things like that. You are not to blame."

"That's easy to say. You weren't there. I've got to go." He started for the fishing gear.

"I'll get it."

"I've got my car—"

"Go. Your client needs you, and this stuff isn't heavy."

Cody jogged toward his vehicle in the parking bay at the end of the pier, with little left for Mrs. Abare.

Early the next morning, Maggie trudged up the stairs to the third floor of City Hall, carrying a sack of doughnuts from Rhonda's Bakery and a cup of coffee for Cody, assuming he wasn't with a client or gone. His door stood open so she crossed the corridor and poked her head inside.

"Good morning." She held up the bag. "I hope you've got an appetite. I've brought you breakfast. Not the most nutritious one but delicious."

"Aah, I'll sacrifice nutrition for flavor. I need the sugar and the coffee." He rose and came from behind his desk.

She moved into his office and passed him the sack and drink. For a second their hands touched. The contact caused her stomach to flutter. She pulled back, needing some separation. She couldn't stop thinking about him last night, wondering how he was doing with so many people needing to talk to him. "How is Mrs. Abare?"

"How did you know?" He knew he hadn't revealed a patient's name, even when taking a call in front of another. "Never mind. I forget things fly around this town faster than the speed of light. She's much better."

"Good. Her daughter told Kim who told me about her falling apart last night. I'm glad you were there for her."

"There needs to be two of me." He checked his watch. "My first client should be here in fifteen minutes."

"Any breaks today?"

"About a half hour to grab lunch."

"Sounds like my kind of day. Ruth and I have one meeting after another to make sure the town is as prepared as it can be. We should know by this evening where it's most likely going to make landfall."

"Yeah, but it is an emotional roller coaster until then."

"Where are you and Hannah going to ride out the hurricane? You're welcome to come with us. My friend said I could bring anyone who needs a place. She has a large house."

"I might send Hannah. I'm going to stay and assist our police."

"Have you ever been through a hurricane?"

"No. But I told the chief I would work the phones for as long as people can call in."

"After Hurricane Naomi I envision a mass exodus."

"I know of some who have already left."

"But like you, there are always some who have to stay. As a nurse and a firefighter, Kathleen and Gideon will have to, but her two sons will come with us."

He sat back against his desk and opened the sack. "Want one?"

"No. I was up early and had my breakfast over an hour ago." She hadn't been able to sleep more than a few hours. Mostly because she couldn't get Cody out of her mind. When she managed, then all she thought about was the last storm. The noises of the wind and rain had filled her mind, pounding her as they both had Hope.

"It sounds like you all have a plan and everything is working out." He took a big bite of his doughnut then a swig of his coffee.

"As much as you can. As with all things weather-related, there's an element of unpredictability. What if Hattiesburg isn't far enough? I'm not worried about my friend's place flooding, but there could still be fierce winds."

"When can we predict the future?"

"Never."

"Then all we can do is make plans and then be ready to change at the last minute."

He was right. No wonder he had a way of calming down a person like Mrs. Abare, even Brady and Keith. She took several steps back. "I'd better go and let you get ready for your first client." At the doorway she turned to leave.

"Maggie."

She peered back. "Yes?"

"I'm grabbing lunch at eleven-thirty. Can you join me?"

She ran through her schedule of meetings and said, "Yes. I have about forty-five minutes around that time. Let me get something for us and we can eat in your office. It's too windy and hot outside."

When she left, she passed his client coming toward his office. Maggie greeted the former mayor and hurried down the hall. The town was in good hands with Cody.

"Look who I found when I went into the café to get some sandwiches." Maggie stepped into Cody's office with Hannah following behind her. "So I brought enough for all three of us."

"What are you doing here?" Cody moved to the round table he had with four chairs.

"Just stopping by for lunch. We secured the

hotel, and I came back to help Zane with some other sites. Maggie persuaded me to have lunch with her and my big brother. Since I haven't seen you in the past couple days, I thought this might be it until everything was over with. You are one busy man."

Maggie sat in between Cody and Hannah. "He was able to take a break and go fishing last night."

"Good for you."

"With my son. Which means it was really work."

"Fun way to have a session, though," Hannah said. "I may have to take up fishing. Well, maybe when my boys are old enough."

For Cody, listening to his sister talk about her soon-to-be-born children hammered home the fact that she would be a mother in a few months. A single mother with limited support. "Have you decided what you're going to do?"

Hannah lowered her gaze, picked up her sandwich and took a bite.

"You're staying, aren't you?" As he asked the question, he held his breath, not wanting to hear her answer.

Hannah nodded, finished chewing and said, "I can't follow you all over the world. I know you usually stay in the United States, but not always. I don't see doing that with two babies in tow. I need a home, even if it's a small apartment. When you're in an area, you have to concentrate on the people who need you. Your time is taken by them. Look what has been happening the past couple days. You come home late, get up early and go back out to meet with your clients."

"It's not that bad. I get some time."

"Not at the beginning or in time of crisis. I need stability—at least as much as you can have with two newborns."

He'd known this would happen and had prepared himself. Or, at least, he thought he had. Now he realized he hadn't. When she'd finished high school and decided to stay in California, he'd felt a loss that had staggered him. It had taken months to slowly, painstakingly fill the void. He'd learned to live totally alone. Until she'd come to Hope, he'd felt content with that lot.

"Cody, I'll be here for her. She'll have help. You won't need to worry about her."

"I'm glad, but..." It wasn't the same thing as him being here for his sister.

What do I do? Leave? Visit occasionally? Lord, what do You want from me? I promised years ago I would help others. Then You gave me this opportunity to work for the Christian Assistance Coalition.

Hannah reached across the table and took his

hand. "It's so much easier to keep in touch with all the technological advances. You can do a live chat on the computer. It's almost like you'll be here." She smiled at him. "I know this is what I have to do. Every time I thought about leaving and moving around like we used to, I got depressed. I think that's why I called Aaron. If he wanted to be a part of his children's lives, I had a good reason to stay or to move back to California."

He didn't know what to say. He could help his clients but not himself. Why was he having such a hard time with this? No answer came, only frustrating him more. He balled the paper napkin in his hand and stared at the half-eaten turkey sandwich. His gut solidified into a rock.

He started to rise when Ruth appeared in the doorway. Her face brightened with a huge smile.

"Hurricane Carl is turning westerly. Hope isn't going to get the full force of the storm."

Relief flooded Hannah's face immediately, but Maggie's forehead knitted. She ate some of her sandwich, avoiding eye contact with him and his sister. Why wasn't she happier?

"We'll have to pray for the people in the path of Carl," he said, sure that was who she was thinking about. She had such a kind heart. She didn't want Hope hit, but neither did she want anywhere else.

"Of course. If it continues to turn to the west,

there is a section where it could strike that won't cause a lot of damage. Not many people live there." Ruth shook her head. "But let's pray that the storm lessens in intensity so no one gets hurt." She backed out of the doorway. "Got to get to the office. I imagine the phones will be ringing off the wall."

Maggie rose. "I can come—"

"Stay. Finish your lunch. We'll be plenty busy this afternoon." Ruth disappeared down the hall.

Maggie sank into her chair and began eating again, her gaze averted.

"I'd better get to the work site where Zane is. He might revise his plans for what he wants us to do." Hannah gathered up her trash, gave Cody a kiss on the cheek and breezed out of the room.

When his sister was gone, he leaned toward Maggie. "What's wrong?"

She lifted her head and looked right at him. "We shouldn't be celebrating too soon. This happened last year and Hurricane Naomi made a U-turn and came right back and hit Hope."

"That's right. I was thinking I would be going to Florida's panhandle. I was surprised by what happened."

She shot to her feet. "I'd better go back to work. Ruth is right. People will be flooding the mayor's office with questions. We're not out of the woods yet."

Before Cody could stand, Maggie hurried out of the office, tossing her trash in the can by the door. Its plunk seemed to vibrate the air as if she were making a statement. Taking a step to go after her, he glanced at his watch. His next appointment would be here any minute. He'd catch her after work.

After cleaning up his lunch, he paused at the window that overlooked the front of City Hall. In the distance he could see the Gulf, gray clouds bellowing in the sky. Concern plagued him. Maggie wasn't doing as well as she stated.

"Yes, Mrs. Abare, that's what the weather channel has said. It has turned more to the west," Maggie said to one of many townspeople who had been calling all afternoon wanting to know what to do. "We recommend you stay informed about what direction the hurricane is taking and not to undo any of your storm preparation until it has hit land."

"Thank you, dear. That's what my daughter said and Dr. Weston. I feel so much better because of that young man. Good day."

As she hung up, Maggie spied another client going into Cody's office at six o'clock. Obviously others felt as she did. They were vulnerable to

Hurricane Carl. Cody was giving out the official advice—stay informed and prepared.

The light on Ruth's phone was lit so she was still talking to the police chief. She'd stay to see how long Ruth needed her. But at least the calls weren't as frequent. Leaning back in her chair, Maggie closed her eyes and inhaled a lungful of air. No matter what she feared, she had to be calm for Uncle Keith and Brady.

The ring of the phone jarred her straight up. She grappled for the receiver and said, "The mayor's office, Maggie Sommerfield speaking."

"Maggie, are you okay?"

The cold piece of plastic she held nearly slipped from her fingers. She tightened her hold and replied, "Why are you calling, Dad?"

Chapter Thirteen

"I heard about Hurricane Carl this morning and wanted to see how you were doing," Maggie's father said.

How do you think? Lousy. But Maggie kept those words to herself. She should have expected this from her father. The only other times he had called was when her mother had died a couple years ago and then again when Hurricane Naomi had hit. It took a disaster for him to contact her. Otherwise, anytime she'd talked to him had been because she had initiated it.

"Maggie? Are you there?"

"Yes."

"I know we haven't talked in a while, but I wanted you to know I was thinking about you and the people in Hope."

"You don't need to worry about the town. I

think the hurricane is going to hit somewhere else. At least that's what the National Weather Service is now saying." But he wouldn't know that because he didn't really care enough to keep track once he found out about the storm. "I'm sorry, Dad, but I have a lot to do. Goodbye."

She hung up, still hearing his deep baritone voice. When the phone rang again, Maggie ignored it in case it was him. She couldn't talk to him now and pretend that they had a normal relationship, that he hadn't gone along with Mom and cut her out of his life. The memory pierced her with a shaft of pain. She buried her face in her hands and fought to forget.

"Maggie, the phone was ringing." Ruth came to the doorway into her office. "That was your father. I told him you were gone. I thought you'd left."

She raised her head, her throat clammed with emotions she wanted to deny. "I talked to him a few minutes ago."

"Oh. Are you okay?"

"Yes." She fumbled in her drawer for her purse. "Is it all right if I leave?"

"Sure."

Maggie rose and rushed out of the office. *He doesn't get to act like the caring father now after thirteen years.*

* * *

Maggie entered the house by the front door, hoping she could escape to her room undetected. She crossed to the stairs.

"Where have you been?" Uncle Keith asked from the living room entrance. "Ruth said you left the office over an hour ago. I was worried something had happened."

Hand on the newel post, Maggie glanced back at her uncle. "I went for a drive. I'm sorry I worried you." Her fingers tightened their grip on the wooden railing.

"What did my brother have to say?"

"You talked to him? When?"

"This afternoon. He called here wanting to talk to you."

Her throat thickened. For the last hour she'd driven along the coast with no destination in mind. She'd ended up getting out of her car and walking on the beach. The wind blew, the waves bigger than usual. But no matter how much she had wanted to find some kind of peace, she couldn't.

"I'm gathering by your silence it didn't go well," her uncle said.

"Did you expect it to? We've talked a handful of times since he and Mom left Hope more than a decade ago. I didn't even know Mom was sick or that she'd died until after the funeral."

"Would it have made any difference to you?"

The question hit her in the chest, ripping through her heart. She sank to the stairs, tears she hadn't been able to shed burning her eyes. "Yes." The word came out unexpectedly. She'd always thought it hadn't made any difference, but it did. She'd needed to say goodbye to her mother. She hadn't with Robbie—not really.

Uncle Keith sat beside her on the step. "I told John he needed to tell you about why your mother was the way she was, but he didn't want you to know. I'm not sure why. Pride. Some kind of loyalty to Marilyn. I can't answer that. I do know he loved Marilyn to distraction."

"I know, but I'd hoped he'd have some love for me."

"He did—in his own way. Marilyn has been gone for almost two years and he's just started to pull his life together. To join the living again. I know what he's going through. I did the same when my first wife died. I thought everything was over with. Slowly I realized it wasn't, and then I found Ruth, who was able to show me there was more to life than what I'd been going through."

Her fingers threaded together, and she closed

her eyes, willing her tears away. "What story should Dad have told me?"

"That your mother was pregnant with you before they were married. She wanted to have you and give you up for adoption. She was eighteen and didn't want to get married or have children. Your dad talked her into marrying him. Even though she grew to love your father more every day, I could tell she resented you. It broke my heart. John spent his whole life trying to make it up to her, for staying with him, but I don't think she was ever really happy." He covered her hands with one of his. "You've become like a second daughter to me."

A tear fell and splashed onto his wrist. "Is that supposed to help me? How?"

"Because you need to know the truth before you can fully deal with it. And don't tell me it doesn't bother you. It does. You dad wants to come back to Hope. I think he wants your forgiveness."

Maggie scrambled to her feet and faced her uncle. "No, he can't come back."

"Why not?"

"Because he left me—disowned me. You don't get a second chance to—" She couldn't say the rest of the words: *hurt her.*

Whirling around, she rushed to the front door

and wrenched it open. Outside on the veranda, she scanned the area, searching for some place to escape from the world.

That evening as the sun began to set, Cody sat on his balcony, his cell in his pocket in case someone needed to get in touch with him. But for the moment, he relished the quiet as he noticed people coming and going at a leisurely pace—not the frantic one of the last couple days as they had prepared for the hurricane. The latest news from the U.S. Weather Bureau confirmed that Hurricane Carl had changed its course more westerly with no hint of turning back.

Why do I keep thinking I need to stay, Lord? Is that what You want me to do? For the past two days, I've met with so many people who needed me—not just because of the hurricane. How do I walk away from them?

How can I walk away from Maggie? I love her. I tried not to, but I do. What do I do about it?

When she ran out of his office today, he wanted to go after her, but then he'd had one client after another. When he'd finally had time to think, he didn't know what to say to Maggie. Until he knew his own heart.

Hannah pulled up to the curb and climbed from her car. Waving to him, she strode toward the stairs. He couldn't turn his back on his only immediate family. That much he knew. And when he thought that, a peace descended, nothing about this decision nagging him not to do it.

Hannah opened the balcony door. "Whatcha doing out here?"

"Thinking, now that I've had some quiet time."

"Will you be okay about my decision? I've thought long and hard over it, and I think it's for the best."

"I agree."

Her eyebrows lifted. "You do?" She took the other chair. "I'm glad you aren't upset at me anymore."

"I haven't been upset with you but with myself."

"Why?"

He stared at his sister who looked so much like their mother. "When Mom died, I promised myself I would be here for you."

"You have been, but I'm a big girl now. I can take care of myself."

"I know that. After Mom's death, I went to a dark place. I begged God to take my pain away, that I'd do anything to help others if only I didn't hurt so much. And He did."

She snapped her fingers. "Just like that."

"Not exactly, but over time, I was able to deal with Mom's loss. I decided then I would help others, that the Lord gave me another chance." He took a deep breath, laced with the scent of the sea nearby. "I'm staying in Hope. I have a place where I can still help others, but be here for you, too."

"Don't stay because of me. I don't want to be the one that you stay for. I'll be okay."

"I know you'll be okay, but don't tell me you don't want your sons to have an uncle in their life."

"I can't say that. I do, but no matter where you are, you'll be their uncle and I'll make sure they know that."

He rose, bent down and kissed her cheek. "I know you will. And I love you for that. You are not going to talk me out of this." He turned toward the door.

"Where are you going?"

"To see Maggie."

"You love her, don't you?"

"Yeah. I'm going to put myself out there again. If I don't, I'll always regret it."

"Good, it's about time you woke up."

He chuckled. "You're right. It has been like I've been sleeping through life. Or at the least watching from the sidelines."

* * *

Darkness approached, and all Maggie could think about was that her mother hadn't wanted her. She'd known that but to hear it confirmed squeezed her heart until the pain encompassed her whole being. She felt as though she'd been left all over again. Seated on the beach across from Bienville, she clasped her arms around her raised knees.

"Maggie."

She tensed. Had Uncle Keith called Cody to come over and talk to her? She was beyond that.

Cody sat beside her. "Keith told me you were out here."

"Go home. I'm not one of your clients. You didn't have to come. I'll be all right."

"Will you? Take it from a guy who has avoided facing my problems, it isn't going to work."

She slanted a glance at him. "You have problems? I thought you had your whole life mapped out. You go from one place to the next because that way you won't have to deal with feelings. They can be so nasty at times." Even over the sound of the sea, she could hear him suck in a deep breath.

His gaze clashed with hers. "I'm not leaving here. I want to help you."

She swung her attention to the last wave that

broke over the sand a few feet from her. Anger shouted for release. "Don't you dare come here and try to analyze my feelings. You avoid your own so you don't have a right to mine."

She tried to stand, but Cody clamped a hand about her arm and held her still. "Contrary to what you think, I do have feelings. I came over to tell you a few of them. That's when Keith told me your dad called and you were upset."

She shook off his touch. "I'm beginning to think you have it right. Retreat from everyone. Keep yourself protected by not letting anyone in. It's a lot less messy."

"I was wrong."

"No, you weren't."

"Yes, I was. You can do that for a while, but when you least expect it—in my case coming to Hope, to what I thought would be a routine assignment—emotions come flooding back. I thought if I could shut off my feelings and be an observer, I could do my job, move on to the next one and be content. I'm not anymore."

"Why not?"

"Because Hope has a way of insinuating itself into a person's life—at least mine. These past few days, I discovered I can't walk away and not leave part of myself here. I've come to care for the people of Hope but especially for you."

Maggie dropped her arms from around her legs and angled toward him. "Me? What are you saying?"

"I'm telling you, Maggie Sommerfield, that I don't want to leave. You've made it clear you won't leave Hope, and you know what? I understand why. I want to stay because of you."

He would regret it later and blame her. She wouldn't be responsible for that. "No, you can't stay. I won't let you. You need to do what you do best. I saw recently how much you help others. I think that's because you know what it's like to lose someone in a disaster. You've been through it. You can identify with us."

"Others can, too. The people who work for Christian Assistance Coalition are great. They know what they're doing. But there are people who need *me* here." He brushed his fingers down her jaw. "Didn't you tell me once I should think of opening a practice here on the coast?"

"Yes, but I was wrong." Her panic mushroomed. Her father had forced her mother to do something she didn't want to do and look what happened to that. "No, you should leave. We're going to be fine. The hurricane is going toward the northern Mexican coast where it will do minimum damage. It's even losing steam, slowing down."

"What are you really afraid of?"

"I won't have you blame me for you doing something you didn't really want to do. Hannah will be fine. We are becoming good friends, so you won't need to worry about her. You know I'm a woman of my word. So see, there's no real reason you should stay."

"Yes, there is."

"What?"

"You. I love you."

"But—"

He cupped his hand behind her neck and tugged her toward him. He settled his mouth on hers while wrapping his arms around her and pressing her against him. She wanted to resist but couldn't. She embraced him and thought for a few seconds she would relish his lips on hers, then she would end it. Go on with her life.

But seconds evolved into a minute, and the kiss deepened, pulling to the surface all the needs she had suppressed since Robbie had left her. Her emotions poured into her response to him. She couldn't hide her feelings for him any longer.

"I love you, Cody, but I want you to be happy doing what you need to do."

He leaned back, framing her face. A blue fire smoldered in his eyes. "I am. All I wanted to do was help others, but I got locked into the same pattern I had been doing my whole life. I thought God wanted me to travel from disaster to disaster doing what I could, but that was my guilt speaking. I thought if I did, it would make up for my mother dying in the tornado because of me. Until lately, I haven't been able to forgive myself for doing something childish when I *was* a child. Now I realize we can't control certain circumstances. When things happen beyond our control, we need to acknowledge that, not dump guilt on ourselves."

She clasped his hands, the warmth of his palms searing his mark on her. Forever.

"I won't abandon you, Maggie. I love you. I want to spend the rest of my life with you. I want to have a family. I want to enjoy being with my nephews and sister. And if I can help people in this area along the way, then I'll be blessed."

Her love swelled into her throat, tearing her eyes. She swallowed several times before she managed to say, "That is the most beautiful thing a person has said to me."

His mouth stretched into a smile. "Good. Because you'll hear it a lot. I've held back my emotions for so long. Now all I want to do is pour them out."

She traced his lips. "I'm thinking it might take

you a while to get use to expressing your feelings, but I'm patient."

The dim light of dusk blanketed the beach. Cody slung his arm around her and plastered her against his side. "This is one of the things I enjoy about Hope. The beach at sunrise and sunset."

She cushioned her head on his shoulder. "I know Brady will be happy you're staying. Ruth and Uncle Keith, too."

"Speaking of Keith, what are you going to do about your father? Keith has a point. You have to deal with him and the situation. As I said, avoiding it won't work in the end."

"I know what I have to do."

"Forgive him?"

"Yes. If I want to be free, I have to. Carrying this anger around inside me is only harming me in the long run. I'm not going to keep doing it."

"What if he moves back here? Wants to be a part of your life? Brady's?"

"I'll deal with that when it happens. Mom wasn't an easy person to live with. But he loved her."

"He's been by himself for a while now. Maybe he's come to realize loving someone isn't always about agreeing with them one hundred percent."

Maggie chuckled. "I guess I can count on you to tell me if I'm doing something wrong."

"That goes two ways. It was you who demanded I feel, let people in. I had to be taught to participate in life again." He lifted her chin so she could look at him. "And you were an excellent teacher."

She reached up and dragged his mouth to hers, then proceeded to show him how much she loved him.

Epilogue

"Grandpa is here," Brady yelled from the foyer of Bienville.

In the kitchen, Maggie tensed. Her heartbeat hammered against her rib cage. Standing at the sink, she closed her eyes and inhaled a soothing breath.

Large hands clasped her shoulders and kneaded them. "You will be all right. With our wedding in a week, we're starting a new life." Cody kissed the side of her neck. "What a nice way to start a new relationship with your dad."

"I know and I have forgiven him." She turned around to face her fiancé. Cradling her hand along his jaw, she peered into his eyes so full of love. "I'm putting my past behind me."

"*We* are putting our past behind us." His lips whispered across hers. "Let's go greet your dad."

Taking his hand in hers, Maggie strode toward

the foyer. Brady was staying only for a few minutes before he went to football practice at the school.

Her dad's gaze latched on to hers and a smile crinkled the corners of his eyes. But he remained where he was, a few feet inside the entrance. "Maggie, you're looking good." He flicked his attention to Brady. "And your son is all grown up. The last time I saw him he was just a toddler."

"Grandpa, I've got to go, but I'll be back for dinner. Football practice will be starting soon. I'm a receiver."

"Can't wait to see you play." Her dad slapped her son on the back, then gave him a hug. "I'll see you later. I'll be here."

As Brady left, Cody moved forward and held out his hand to shake her dad's. "It's nice to finally meet you in person."

Her father looked Cody up and down. "I've heard good things about you from my brother."

Maggie stared at her father, unsure what to do or say after all this time, even though they had talked on the phone at least once a week since that first call in August. Tears shone in her dad's eyes, matching the ones glistening in hers. "Dad, I'm glad you're in Hope."

"I didn't want to miss your wedding."

With Cody by her side, his arm around her

shoulders, she thought of the fresh start she had with Cody and now with her dad. No more feelings of abandonment. No more fear of showing another person what she felt. No more anger over the past.

Her dad shifted from one foot to the other. "I wish I'd never left, but I loved your mother and she wanted to go back home to Arizona to be near her family. It's taken me almost two years since her death to pull my life together, to figure out what I wanted."

"What do you want?"

"My family—you and Brady."

Her heart expanded with his words. She leaned forward and kissed his cheek. "C'mon into the kitchen. Cody is helping me make a German chocolate cake, his favorite."

Her dad looked at Cody. "I think we're gonna get along just fine. That's my favorite, too."

Cody pressed Maggie to his side. "I didn't have any worries about us not getting along. After all, we both love Maggie."

"That we do, son."

She laughed. "Y'all gonna make me blush."

Cody brushed his fingertip across her cheek, then gave her a brief kiss. "Honey, there's no *make* about it. You are blushing."

* * * * *

Dear Reader,

In *A Mom's New Start* I explore the dynamics of different families. Maggie is a single mother (never married). Cody became a "parent" to his little sister when his parents died. Kim and Zane are married, and Zane is a stepfather to Anna, Kim's daughter. Maggie (with her son, Brady) is part of an extended family, living with her uncle and his wife. There are so many different types of family nowadays. What the average family looks like is changing. Often members of a family live hundreds of miles from others in their family. There aren't as many families where three or four generations live in the same household, or close to each other. Staying close to our loved ones who live states away can be a challenge, but keeping in touch with family is important.

I love hearing from readers. You can contact me at margaretdaley@gmail.com or at 1316 S. Peoria Ave. Tulsa, OK 74120. You can also learn more about my books at www.margaretdaley.com. I have a quarterly newsletter that you can sign up for on my website or you can enter my monthly drawings by signing my guest book on the site.

Best wishes,

Margaret Daley

Questions for Discussion

1. Cody helped others get through their problems, but he had shut himself off from others as his way of coping. He moved from place to place, never staying long to form friendships. Even if you move a lot because of your circumstances, how can you make friends and connect with others? Is it important to have someone you can talk to about your problems? Why or why not?

2. Who is your favorite character? Why?

3. In this story, the importance of forgiving is explored. Why is it important to forgive others and ourselves? What happens when we live in the past rather than looking forward to the future? Which do you focus on—past, present or future? Why?

4. Cody tried to have a long-distance relationship with a woman he was in love with. Can that kind of relationship work out? If so, how? If not, why doesn't it? What are things a couple can do if they find themselves separated by distance for a time? How do they stay close?

5. What is your favorite scene? Why?

6. Maggie had her son out of wedlock. Her choice led to repercussions that hurt her and her family. Have you ever made the kind of decision that you felt you paid for more than most? How did you deal with it?

7. Brady felt he had no control in his life. He suffered from depression. He didn't realize there are a lot of things we can't control, but that we can control our reactions to them. What are some things that have happened to you lately that have been out of your control? How did you react to them?

8. Maggie loved to knit and participated in the Shawl Ministry. Her shawls went to people who needed to be comforted as they went through a difficult illness or event in their life. What are some hobbies you do? How are they important to you?

9. Maggie was trying to rebuild her life as well as her extended family's after the hurricane. She thought she had dealt with the disaster and its aftermath until another hurricane threatened to hit Hope. It was the final straw. She fell apart. Have you ever had continual

setbacks like that? If so, how did you deal with them? What got you through it?

10. Maggie didn't realize she'd held some resentment toward her fiancé for re-upping in the service against her wishes, leading to his death. She knew God wanted her to forgive and move on, but she had a hard time doing that. Have you ever done something you know you shouldn't? How did the situation turn out?

11. This is a series about hope in a time of tragedy. What are ways you can give hope to another in his time of need?

12. Depression can be serious. A lot of teens suffer from it as Brady did. Do you know a loved one who has suffered from depression? How do you help them cope with it? What were some suggestions you gave them about coping with depression?

13. Cody felt responsible for his mother's death in a tornado. She was killed when she was coming to pick him up. If she hadn't been in the wrong place at the wrong time, she would be alive. He promised God he would help others through a crisis if He would take his

pain away. Have you ever promised God to do something if He did something in return? How did it work out for you?

14. Maggie didn't want to leave her hometown. It was her haven. Cody didn't understand that, since he'd never experienced it. Maggie felt a home was a physical place, whereas Cody felt it was in a person's mind (a mental place). Which do you think it is? Why do you think that?

15. When her fiancé died and her parents disowned her, Maggie was scared to trust in a relationship after being hurt twice. She felt abandoned. Her past ruled her life. Do you have something in your past that has done that to you? How can you get past it?

LARGER-PRINT BOOKS!

GET 2 FREE
LARGER-PRINT NOVELS
PLUS 2 FREE
MYSTERY GIFTS

Love Inspired®

Larger-print novels are now available...

LILP11B